Books by Claire Logan

Ring-A-Ding Dead!
The Vanishing Valet!
A New Year's Shot!

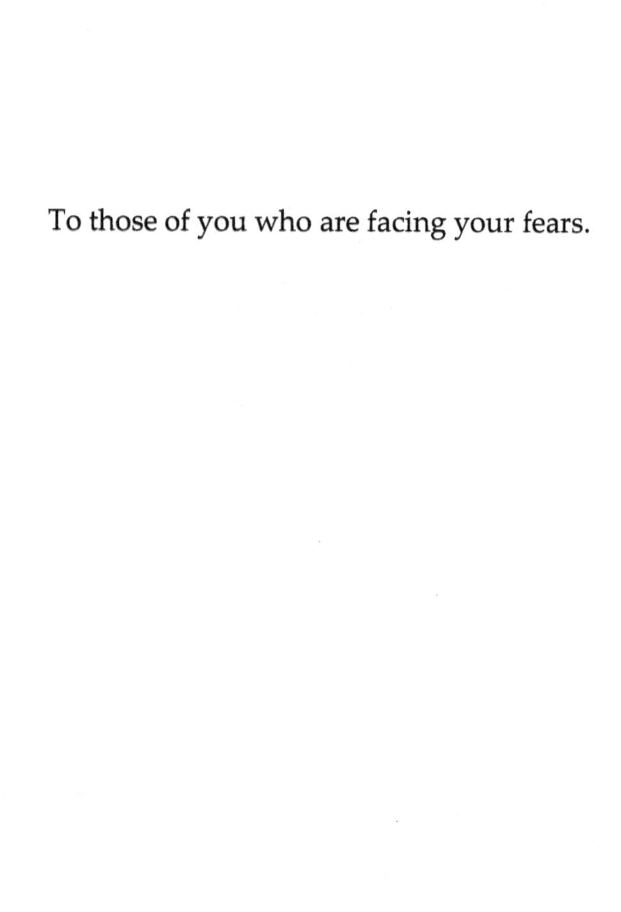

To those of you who are facing your fears.

A New Year's Shot!

The Myriad Mysteries #3

Claire Logan

Preface

This is not historical fiction. It's cozy mystery! In that regard, certain details known to the early 1920s in Chicago (radio call signs, business names, etc.) have been altered, and are not typographical errors.

Also, cozy mysteries should be fun! Just as regular people would never be involved with homicide investigations in real life, I do realize that my dear couple are living an idyllic life, unlikely to be seen in real 1920s Chicago.

So if you're looking for ugly historical realities, gentle reader, please look elsewhere.

1

It was well past dinner. Dressed for bed, Mr. Hector Jackson and his wife Pamela sat on the floor of his spacious bathroom in the Myriad Hotel beside their black toy poodle Bessie and her five puppies.

The little dogs nestled in a soft thick blanket under the sink, the edges tucked under so the blanket made a raised ring around the new family. A second, matching blanket, had been threaded through the pipes below the sink to make a canopy of sorts for the new little family's bed. The puppies hadn't opened their eyes yet, and wobbled towards the scent of their mother.

Their sire must have been a deep golden brown: one puppy was black, one golden, one black and golden spotted, and two were shades of brown in between. They'd be beautiful animals when grown.

"They're still so little," his wife said.

This made him smile. He petted Bessie's curly black hair. "So they are."

Mr. Jackson leaned back, laying his hand upon the black and white tile. He'd been in Chicago months already and never noticed that his bathroom floor was heated! He wondered how they did it. "A perfect place for such small animals on a chilly night."

His wife giggled, snuggling up beside him. "Indeed it is. Although we need a blanket of our own. This floor's quite hard."

He clambered to a standing position, then held his hand out to hoist his wife up beside him. Looking down at the puppies, he sighed. "They won't stay so small for long. And we can't keep them here." Small and well-mannered as Bessie was, in a hotel suite one dog was quite enough.

"I know. I know." She cleared her throat. "A pity. I wish one day we might have land, and a place we could keep puppies like these ones."

He shrugged. "I have a few places like that. But not here in Chicago."

At that, she laughed. "I suppose we could buy one. But I'm not quite ready to become a farmer's wife in the snow just yet."

He thought the idea of being a farmer rather amusing. He'd never once considered such a thing. A mansion, perhaps, or some villa overlooking the sea. "And here I thought you liked Chicago."

"I do!" She took a deep breath, let it out. "I love being here, with my friends, the gardens, the nightlife." She beamed down at the dogs. "I love my little Bessie." Then she twitched a bit, and looked up at him. "And you, too, of course."

He laughed. "I suppose I should be glad I rate! Even if it's at the end of the list."

She poked his side, grinning. "But I was referring to here. I can be with you anywhere."

A great fondness for her came over him, and he put his arm around her. "That you can. Anywhere in the world you desire, dear girl, I'll gladly go with you."

She beamed at him, fitting herself into his side. The couple moved from the bathroom turned puppy-house, towards his bedroom, everything neatly arranged by his valet and their floor's maid.

This was the kind of life he loved. He loved the feel of thick black carpeting on his bare feet, the fresh smell of the newly cleaned rooms. He loved the golden flame-shaped radiators, the telephone in their rooms, how everything was kept in such order.

And he loved not having to do any of it himself.

They went through his bedroom into their suite's parlor, where a fire crackled still. His wife ventured to the French doors, peering out through the glass, past the balcony, into the darkened streets. "They say it's supposed to be warmer tomorrow." She glanced at him over her shoulder. "For the holiday."

He laughed. "Warmer in winter here means not too terribly icy." He sat at the large wooden table. "Let's see. Who might want a puppy?"

Mr. Lee Francis, the Myriad Hotel's Head Clerk, had already chosen the black-and-gold spotted one — when the pup was weaned, of course — for his wife and baby son. But that left four to give away.

They'd already asked around a bit. His pal George Neuberg — the Myriad's new Headwaiter — was gone from his little apartment most of the day. His wife's friend Ophelia Denton — a showgirl at the Club Patruni — lived in a boarding house, no pets allowed.

His wife's voice broke his reverie. "Did you ask any of the maids?"

"Anyone here all day would be here all day," he said. "Not the ideal situation."

Bessie came trotting out, went to him and put her feet on his leg, whining.

"I'll call for one of the boys to come walk her," his wife said, going to the telephone. Bessie followed her.

They'd bought a wrap for Bessie's midsection to keep her teats warm in the chilly weather, so he fetched it from his closet and put it on her. By this time, the boy had arrived: the eldest one, perhaps fifteen. He tipped his cap to them, then looked down, arms wide. "Bessie!"

From the way she danced, the little dog seemed just as happy to see him.

Mr. Jackson smiled fondly at the pair going off down the hall. "What a wonderful place we live in!"

He felt his wife's arm going round his waist. "Indeed we do."

The couple sat on the sofa in front of the fire while they awaited Bessie's return.

Mr. Jackson felt more than a bit anxious about the coming holiday, most particularly, the thought of their friends out on the town. But he didn't know how to broach the matter to his wife.

Finally, he decided the best course of action was to speak of it directly. "We have to tell them the truth. As much of it as we can."

"Oh?"

He sighed. "It's dangerous for them to be kept in the dark much longer."

Her eyes were huge in the firelight. "Because of the Feds."

When he'd brought her to this place, she'd been running from a life that had fallen into shambles in a truly horrible way. He'd sworn to protect her, a vow he could never break — even if he didn't love her in a way he'd never loved any woman before. "It's the safest course of action."

His wife said, "It's none of their business."

"It is, and you know it. What if —"

She cried out, "I don't want either of them to know!"

"It's not fair for them **not** to. What if one of these places gets raided? What if they're taken in? Questioned?"

Fear touched her eyes, and he hated it that he should be the one to put that there, when finally she'd found a place to be happy. "My darling, please. Listen to me. They're both fine people. They care about us. But they wouldn't know what to say, or more importantly, what not to. It would grieve them if they were to harm us by some innocent comment." He leaned forward to peer into her eyes. "They'd be furious that we didn't warn them. And the longer we keep this from them, the more likely they'll learn the truth from someone else. They'd be hurt, feeling that we didn't trust them. Wonder what **else** we've hidden."

Her eyes fell.

"I love you." He reached over, lifted her chin, and tears stood in her eyes. "I love you more than anything in this world. I left everything for you: my home, my titles, my family. I would die, right now —"

She flinched.

"— before I let anything happen to you. I would take you right this minute and leave everything and everyone I have here before I allowed anyone to bring you back there. I'm on your side. Do you understand?"

She flung herself upon his chest sobbing, and he held her close, stroking her black curly hair.

"Shh," he said finally, as her sobbing turned to coughing, then to quiet tears. "All will be well, dear girl. All will be quite well."

2

The next morning, Mrs. Jackson felt better. And as she crept out of her Mr. Jackson's room, across the parlor, and into her own bedroom, she decided that he was right. She was thirty years old now, a woman full-grown, not some pampered child.

Secrets had been what got her into this mess. And she'd hidden from her friends long enough. Everyone involved needed to be told, before this all got out of hand.

But what would they think of her? Would they assume her to be a fiend, some deranged murderess who fled rather than face her crimes?

Most of what had happened was all too public. But the worst of it happened in private, betrayals by people she trusted and loved.

Her Mr. Jackson was right: George and Ophelia were good people. But in their shock and dismay over the news, would they go to the Feds themselves?

As the sky began to lighten, a knock came at her bedroom door. "Mrs. Knight! How lovely to see you."

Mrs. Octavia Knight, a professional lady's maid, came in and took off her hat and coat. "As you, ma'am. I hope you slept well?"

"I did."

Mrs. Knight began drawing a bath at once.

Instead of arriving at nine, Mrs. Knight now would examine the Almanac and arrive an hour before sunrise each day. In this way, Mrs. Jackson might be ready to help Monsieur — the Myriad Hotel's young Head Chef — with his rooftop kitchen gardens at dawn.

When Mrs. Jackson first arrived, she'd truly needed Mrs. Knight's help. But now, it was just nice to see the woman, chat about nothing for a bit, and be able to provide a bit of help to her in return. Mrs. Knight had an ill husband and a daughter almost out on her own, and Mrs. Jackson felt sure the extra money came in handy.

As Mrs. Jackson soaked in the tub, she said, "What might you think if a friend told you something terrible? About themselves."

Mrs. Knight hung a long-sleeved woolen forest green day dress upon the bathroom's clothes stand. "I'd feel grateful for her trust in me."

Mrs. Jackson hadn't considered that. And she recalled what Mr. Jackson had said. Would Ophelia be hurt that she hadn't told her sooner? Feel she didn't trust her?

"If she'd been a friend," Mrs. Knight said, "a real friend, and she regretted what she'd done, and was trying to be a better person, to truly change, then I'd have nothing to fear, now, would I?"

"True." Mrs. Jackson washed out her hair, got up from the warm water. The towels here were so beautifully thick and soft. "You've been very helpful."

It was lovely to have Mrs. Knight dry her hair for her before she went out into the cold. The Hotel had an electric hair dryer in the room, but it was rather heavy.

Mrs. Knight moved a stray bit of hair into place. "There! All ready for the day."

Mrs. Jackson smiled at her. "Thank you. We'll be staying in tonight, so enjoy your evening."

"Will you be needing me in the morning?"

"No, you take tomorrow morning off. My treat. Spend some time with your family."

"You're very kind, ma'am. Tomorrow at seven, then?"

Mrs. Knight also took care of her clothing and dressed her for dinner. "Right you are," Mrs. Jackson said. "I'll call if anything changes."

Mrs. Knight smiled fondly at her. "You have a wonderful day."

***

When the elevator reached the roof, Mrs. Jackson stepped onto the roof and unclipped Bessie's leash. The little dog immediately went to the paneled wall beside the elevator shaft to relieve herself. As the elevator closed, Mrs. Jackson took in the glorious sunrise, the crisp cold air, the beautiful blue sky.

And she coughed.

Taking one last drag from her cigarette, she stepped upon it, coiled up Bessie's leash into the pocket of her overcoat, and moved forward. As usual, Bessie began sniffing the entire rooftop.

The rooftop of the Myriad Hotel was as grand and spacious as its inside: fine stone tile paved the way. Large boxes spread across this end of the rooftop, in this area raised to knee high, all carved with intricate patterns. The boxes held dirt and many plants covered in oiled canvas to protect them from the bitter cold.

The young Monsieur already worked there, cutting off a row of cabbages one by one with quick strokes of his knife, then gently placing them, leaves and all, into the low wheeled cart beside him. A young man of average height with black hair and pale blue eyes, Monsieur was a culinary prodigy, his name and portrait gracing more than one of the many magazines here. Since coming here as Head Chef, the Myriad Hotel's restaurant had never fared better, and reservations for those not staying in the Hotel were at a premium.

She felt a great fondness for the young man, waving at him cheerfully when he glanced up. He merely nodded as she passed by.

Mrs. Jackson knelt beside the cart to select a knife on the rack at its end similar to the one he bore. "How many more of these do we need?"

He sliced through the stem of one. "This should be enough." He returned the knife to its holder. "Let's dig the parsnips next."

Fetching long thin trowels, they went down long rows to an area where the boxes stood waist high and found a box entirely full of parsnips. After breaking through the frosty earth on top, they began to wiggle free one fat pale carrot-shaped root at a time. These went in a basket on top of the cabbages.

"If I might ask, sir: what's Paris like? I've never been."

Monsieur's face broke into a rare smile. "Lovely, especially in the spring. I particularly enjoyed walking near the river."

"Do you think you might ever wish to return?"

He shrugged. "It's a crowded place, even more so than here. Perhaps one day, if only to visit friends. I have many there from my days in the Cordon Bleu." He smiled to himself, perhaps recalling some fond memory. "But we write often." He took a foot-long parsnip from the dirt. "It's been terribly busy of late, but once I get some men properly trained, I might be able to plan a holiday. During the Hotel's slow season, of course."

She coughed, and it rattled her chest a bit.

Monsieur peered at her gravely. "I hope all is well?"

"Why yes," she said. "Oh, you mean this cough? It's nothing; merely a tickle."

"Good," he said. "For some, cold air is good for the constitution. For others, it causes illness. My younger sister was one such, and it gave her no end of trouble when she was small." A few of his men had emerged upon the rooftop, and he gestured for them to take the cart. "Let's get the young greens together for today."

In the far area behind the elevator shaft stood a extensive greenhouse. Inside were rows of various plants under glass, including an assortment of young lettuces. Monsieur took up a basket as large as a tire under one arm, restng it upon a cart. Then he began clipping whole handfuls of the small leaves, tossing them in the basket.

"I remember your sister," Mrs. Jackson said. "Have you heard from her?"

"Not in some time," Monsieur said gravely. "They sent her out West, if you recall."

Mrs. Jackson remembered her, a pretty little girl with dark hair. The dry air out West was said to be good for the health. "Well, if you do, please give her my regards!"

Monsieur smiled at her. "I most certainly will."

***

Mr. Jackson woke at the knock on his bedroom door. Putting on a robe, he went to answer.

His manservant (here they called the man a "valet") Mr. Norman Vienna stood there. A lovely young man with light skin and brown hair.

Rather a bit like George, if he was to say. He hadn't considered it before. "Come in. How was your honeymoon?"

"We had a marvelous time, sir, thank you for asking."

"I appreciate you coming in on the holiday."

"Not at all, sir." He gave a sheepish smile. "To be honest, I've been away long enough." He began going through Mr. Jackson's closet. "Rather enjoyed myself, but the bills come in soon."

Mr. Jackson laughed. "Quite so."

Mr. Vienna went into the bathroom, and the sound of water came forth. When he emerged, he said, "Congratulations on the puppies!"

Mr. Jackson felt amused. "Thank you, sir. If you're interested in one, we have four to give away."

Mr. Vienna laughed. "Oh, I don't think the wife would be pleased at that. Not at all. She's not fond of animals." He went to the dresser, retrieving and laying out a clean shirt atop it.

"Pity. But not everyone is. They're a lot of work!"

Mr. Vienna glanced over at him, then moved to the closet. "Going out today, or just the Hotel?"

The Myriad Hotel had any number of amusements — one might never leave it! "I hadn't planned! Perhaps something suitable for both."

Mr. Vienna nodded, his eyes upon the clothing. Then he selected a dark brown tweed suit. "Just the thing! Not too much for breakfast downstairs, yet warm enough for going out. If the weather turns bad, just pop upstairs and fetch your overcoat."

"Splendid!"

Mr. Vienna straightened the bed a bit then laid the suit atop it. "I'll see to your bath, then, sir."

After a nice warm bath and a shave, Mr. Jackson felt much improved. By the time he'd dressed, the door to his wife's bedroom opened, and he heard the sound of little Bessie rushing across the parlor. The little dog hurried past them and to her pups.

"A conscientious mother, that one." Mr. Vienna helped Mr. Jackson into his coat and began to brush it.

"She really is. Couldn't have asked for a better dog."

His wife came to the doorway to the parlor and leaned upon the door-frame. Her light brown cheeks were slightly ruddy from the cold outside, her black curls a bit tossed under the forest green cloche she wore.

She looked gorgeous.

Mr. Vienna grinned, giving her a short nod. "I'll leave you to your day, then." He turned to Mr. Jackson. "Tonight, then?"

Mrs. Jackson said, "I told Mrs. Knight we'd be staying in tonight, and tomorrow morning as well."

"Well there you have it," said Mr. Jackson. "Take a bit of a holiday with the wife. Just put it on our bill."

Mr. Vienna's eyes widened. "Thank you, sir!" He bowed. "Tomorrow night, then. Sir. Ma'am."

"Have a lovely day," his wife called out. Then she went to him and straightened his cravat, which he felt sure didn't need it. "That was very generous of you."

He shrugged, amused. "Remember? Mr. Carlo's been picking up the tab."

3

The upper halls of the Myriad Hotel were the very peak of luxury: marble floors, rosewood paneled walls. Fine brass fixtures high on the walls cast warm soothing light upon the way.

A magnificent painting of the lake tossed by a storm hung above a long narrow brass table across from the elevator, with two seats fashioned in rosewood and upholstered in deep blue velvet beside it.

The elevator door was exquisite Art Deco work carved in brass: a valiant man sounding a horn.

Inside, a man in Hotel livery operated the elevator, bringing them to the lobby.

The same marble floors, but in this elevator area, the marble extended also to the walls. Brilliant electric bulbs overhead lit the scene. In the wide grand lobby itself, little shops lay around to the left, surrounded by rosewood paneling and brass trimmings, with Art Deco murals high upon the walls.

People were everywhere: visiting the shops, gazing at the huge fountain the in the center of the room, going in and out of the brass-edged front double doors, ascending and descending the wide staircase to the right. The couple went past the staircase and to the beveled glass dining room doors. Attendants stood by to open the doors for them, and they ventured inside.

Mr. Jackson seldom saw Mr. Montgomery Carlo, the Hotel's owner. But when he and his wife went down for breakfast, the big swarthy man stood near the Headwaiter's station, beside the Myriad's new Headwaiter, George Neuberg.

A slender, fit, tanned young man, George seemed focused on a paper Mr. Carlo held up for him. George glanced up as the couple approached. "Good morning, sir! Your usual table?"

Mr. Jackson nodded, barely holding back a smile. "If it's available." He held out his hand to Mr. Carlo. "A pleasure to see you."

Mr. Carlo hesitated, just a tad, then shook. "Busy here, getting ready for tonight."

"Ah." Now it became clear: New Year's Eve. "A special party, then."

Mr. Carlo was already back to the paper. "Indeed."

George came round. "This way."

Mr. Jackson found the whole dance amusing. He and his wife knew exactly where the table was: they'd been going to it for months now. Yet for them to go on their own would have set everyone aflutter.

As they moved towards the table, Mr. Jackson said, "Hope your family's well." They had been hosted by George's parents numerous times on their yacht.

"Just dandy," George said. "My Pa's just ordered a new car."

Mr. Jackson let out a surprised laugh. "Really."

"A brand new Pierce Arrow Coupe!" He sounded impressed. "Didn't know the old man was making that kind of money."

"Well, people around here do like boats," Mr. Jackson said. "And your father makes some magnificent ones."

When they got to the beautifully set table, and George had seated them, Mr. Jackson said to him, "When would be a good time for a chat?"

"Heh," George said. "After Carlo leaves, to be sure."

"I'll stop by later then."

As George returned to his post, Mr. Jackson looked over at his wife, who was perusing the menu. "Roasted parsnip soup." She turned to him, eyes wide. "We dug those this morning!"

She took such delight in seeing what she'd helped gather appear in the menu for that day. "I'm sure it'll be delicious." The young man who took on the role of Head Chef for this place certainly earned his keep!

One of the new waiters approached, a young fellow almost as dark-skinned as he, taking out a notepad. The man's name-tag read: Floyd. "Care for some drinks?"

"Coffee, heavy cream, if you please," Mr. Jackson said. "The more the better. And no sugar." He turned to his wife. "And you?"

"Tea," she said, as always.

"Right away," Floyd said.

Just then, the Myriad Hotel's most illustrious personage, the dowager Duchess Cordelia Stayman, came through the glass-paneled doors. Going to the Headwaiter's station, she ignored George entirely, and seemed to be mildly lecturing Mr. Carlo on some matter.

But then she followed after George, her lined face lighting up when she saw them. "Oh, Mr. Jackson! And my dear Mrs. Jackson! How lovely to see you!"

After George seated her across the small square table from him and returned to Mr. Carlo, Duchess Cordelia said, "The happiest of New Years to you both."

"That's very kind of you," Mr. Jackson said. "And to you as well."

His wife leaned forward. "I hope you're well."

Duchess Cordelia leaned back with a satisfied smile. "I am. What a perfectly lovely day it is out!"

"Oh," he said. "You've been out and about already?"

"I have," the dowager said. "I take a turn around the park every morning, rain or shine. It's good to get outside once in a while."

Mr. Jackson was reminded of his fitness club membership. Other than the few times he and George had gone to play tennis, he'd quite forgotten it. "I shall keep that in mind."

"Any plans?"

His wife said, "We plan to stay in tonight."

"As do I," the dowager said. "I'm much too old for late nights and parties these days. Besides, the premiere of 'The Love For Three Oranges' broadcasts tonight!

Mr. Jackson wasn't sure what she meant. "Oh?"

"Oh, yes. Haven't you heard? It's the opera broadcasts on KWY."

His wife said, "What's that?"

"Radio, my dear. It sends music right through the air, to this contraption Albert made! Whenever we would travel, we listened to broadcasts all over the world. We finally have a proper station here in Chicago." She beamed, clasping her lined hands together just under her chin. "And they've been playing opera!"

"Oh," Mr. Jackson said, impressed. He very much liked the opera, but hadn't gone in years. Perhaps he'd have to get one of these contraptions made for him.

"Right down at the Civic Auditorium. But I don't have to go there past all the wildness tonight — I can just listen in my room!" She gave him a satisfied grin. "So I am quite settled. A cup of hot cocoa beside the fire with opera and a new book is all the entertainment I need."

Mr. Jackson said, "Would you like to visit the library after breakfast?"

The dowager beamed. "That would be wonderful."

4

Once Mr. Jackson had escorted his wife and the dowager Duchess to the library, he went up to his rooms to check on Bessie. As it turned out, Bessie and her puppies were asleep. So he returned downstairs to the front desk. "I'd like to access my safe, if you please."

The flier he'd secured there lay folded underneath a bound stack of cash — just in case — and his wife's pistol. Mr. Jackson gazed at the pistol for a long moment, then put the flier into his jacket pocket and returned to where George had been. By this time, Mr. Carlo had left, and George appeared to be taking notes.

George glanced up as he approached. "Ah! There you are." The two shook hands. "I hope all's well?"

"Might I have a word? If you're not too busy."

George gave him a fond smile. "Never too busy for you, old chap."

Mr. Jackson followed George to his office, a smallish affair with lots of cabinets and a bit of a desk. George gestured for him to sit, so he did.

George threw himself into his chair. "What's the news?"

How might he begin ...

He pulled out the flier, heart pounding, and opened it. Upon it sat the words "Wanted For Questioning." It also had a portrait of his wife.

George grew very still. "Wait." He glanced up at him. "Is this ... Pamela?" He took the flier, read through it. "Oh," he said. "So this is **her**." He handed it back. "Quite an old photograph, I'd say."

Mr. Jackson realized just then he'd not been breathing. Perhaps others might not recognize her either. He refolded the flier and put it into his pocket.

"So why are you showing me this?"

A wave of relieved fatigue swept over him, and he leaned one elbow on the desk, resting his forehead upon his hand. "Because I'm sorry it took so long for me to tell you. You of all people deserve to know."

George nodded slowly. "Thank you. Really." He seemed to be at a loss for words. Then a laugh burst from him. "It sounds funny, but I feel honored."

Mr. Jackson felt surprised. "Really?"

"I do." He laughed once more. "A lot of shady stuff goes on here, Hector. Quite a lot." He leaned back, putting an ankle over his knee. "It's more than a bit refreshing to see someone in this town who actually tells the truth."

Mr. Jackson let out a weary breath. "I try, George. I always have." Then he felt amused. "Makes keeping your stories straight much easier."

A laugh burst from George. "I daresay! Hey, want another round of tennis? I should be able to find a few hours next week sometime."

Mr. Jackson rose, extending his hand. "I would very much enjoy it."

***

Later, the couple relaxed in the parlor of their suite, along with their dear friend, Miss Ophelia Denton.

Mr. Jackson put more cream into his coffee. The small sounds new puppies make came from his bathroom. It was early yet, and although most of the buildings lay in shadow, the sky outside was still blue. Fireworks echoed through the closed doors to the balcony around the buildings along Lake Shore Drive.

His wife sat quietly, sipping hot lemonade. She'd been particularly quiet since he'd related his discussion with George, which worried him. Mr. Jackson said to Miss Denton, "Where will you ring in the New Year?"

Miss Denton said, "The Green Mill, of course! If we can get a table. If not, we might go to the South Side."

Mr. Jackson said, "So you like jazz, I take it."

Miss Denton beamed. "Ever so much."

Mr. Jackson drank his coffee, which had gone cold. "Too bad George had to work tonight."

Miss Denton laughed, her reddish-blonde curls wagging around her chin. "Goes with the job."

Although being promoted to Headwaiter gave George a much improved income, it also meant he had to work most every holiday night. "Still," Mr. Jackson said, "it's a pity he'll miss the fun."

Miss Denton had been drinking hot tea, but her hand stopped mid-air. "I forgot to tell you!" She put down her teacup. "The girls and I are having dinner downstairs, so we'll see him then. And Georgie said he'd meet up with us after work. We just need to phone with where we are around one or so."

Mrs. Jackson nodded. "I'm glad to hear it, Pet," she said. "You should get out and have some fun."

Miss Denton reached over to take her hand. "My dear Pam. I know how horrible a time this is for you."

Mr. Jackson hoped his wife would reveal more of why this time was so difficult for her. But she merely gave Miss Denton a smile, which never reached her eyes.

He expected the melancholy. She'd lost her husband and son under terrible circumstances, fleeing with him to Chicago that same day.

And it hadn't yet been a year since. Every little thing must remind her of her family. Hoping to change the subject, he said, "However did you get the evening off?"

"Oh!" Miss Denton became more animated. "We got a bunch of new girls in, enough to let one of us have the evening. So the boss had a secret ballot! You had to put in two names you thought deserved it. Of course everyone put in their own. But I got the most votes for the other." She put her hand to her heart. "I can hardly believe I won."

His wife took the younger woman's hand. "Oh, Pet — I can! You're always filling in for the others, and staying late to help clean up. You most certainly deserve it."

Miss Denton blushed, and the look on his wife's face moved him. She loved the girl ever so much.

His wife turned to him with a real smile. "I'll be happy to stay in tonight. Maybe I've grown old." With that, she let out a chuckle. "But the late nights don't appeal to me as much as they once did."

Mr. Jackson smiled at her. "I quite understand the feeling." He leaned forward. "Before you go, Miss Denton, I need to speak with you."

Miss Denton's fine auburn eyebrows rose. "Oh?"

He gave his wife a quick glance. "There's something you should know, tonight of all nights."

Miss Denton giggled. "Okay, Father Time — I'm no innocent!"

That amused him. "It's that the Feds are always around tonight. Just keep out of trouble, if you can."

The young woman shrugged. "As much as anyone. What's this about?"

He sighed, taking the flier once more from his pocket, making sure to cover his wife's real name with his finger as he did.

Miss Denton gasped, glancing from his wife's portrait to him to his wife. "They want you ... for **this**?"

His wife put her face in her hands.

"But why? What do they think you've done?"

"She didn't kill anyone," Mr. Jackson said confidently. "But the Feds think she might have." He glanced at the flier. "I suppose." He looked back at her. "In any case, try not to attract **too** much attention?"

The young woman felt the paper of the flier. "And this is real. This isn't some sort of joke."

Mrs. Jackson's hands fell from her face. "I wish it were. Why do you think we came here?"

Miss Denton let go of the flier and sat quietly for a moment. "Who else knows?"

"Mr. Carlo," Mr. Jackson said. "The fellow who owns this hotel here. Some of his men, I suppose." The man was a minor ruffian in a city full of them. But he was wealthy, which helped a great deal. "I told George about it earlier."

"Well, I don't believe it." Miss Denton took Mrs. Jackson's hand. "That old rag means nothing to me. I'm not going anywhere." Then she laughed. "Except tonight, of course." Miss Denton rose, so they did as well. "I'm off, then!"

Mrs. Jackson said, "So soon?"

"Me and the girls are having a party of our own." She beamed. "Martinis and Maybellinis." A laugh burst from her, and he wondered how much she'd already had to drink today. "We'll be spiffy tonight!"

"Do be careful," Mrs. Jackson said anxiously. "Call us if you need anything."

Miss Denton gave her a fond bemused smile, then leaned over to kiss her cheek. "I will."

Hugs all round, then she was out the door and gone.

The couple moved towards the sofa, but there came a knock on the parlor door. "I'll see who this is," he said. "You go on and relax."

At the door was their new floor maid, Lela, a woman in her later forties with her long brown hair up in a bun. "Good evening, Mr. Jackson! Care to have me set a fire for you?"

"Why, that would be splendid!" He moved aside to let her pass.

"Something told me you'd be staying in tonight," Lela said. She bent over the unlit fire. In a moment, a lovely warm light spread over the logs. "If you need more wood than that there," she pointed to the basket of small logs beside the fireplace, "just give us a ring."

"Will do, thanks."

Once the woman was gone, he sat beside his wife. She rested her head on his shoulder, and he put his arm round her with a contented sigh.

"At least that's over with," his wife said. "I feared so much that Ophelia would ... I don't know. Look differently at me."

"Now why would she do that?"

She sounded a bit dejected. "I don't know."

"Cheer up," he said. "She didn't."

For a while they sat watching the fire. "Another year past." He kissed her forehead. "And look where we are!"

He loved the way she relaxed into him. Just a few months ago, things were very different. This time last year, she'd wanted nothing to do with him. "Yes," she said. "I do love it here. No schedules, no obligations, no one to manage."

"And no one managing **you**." He laughed to himself at a distant memory. He'd not had anyone managing him for some time.

She sat up, facing him. "Yes! That was the worst of it. Not being able to go anywhere without telling someone and getting permission."

He nodded.

She resumed her snuggling into his shoulder. "I must have made everyone mad with frustration over me." She chuckled then. "I would never do what they insisted."

He kissed her curly black hair. "I can imagine." In that, they'd been much the same. Free spirits, they were.

He'd been one of the few who guessed she'd bolt for the station after the horror of that night was said and done. How fortunate that he'd gotten to her before she disappeared forever.

He'd done everything he knew to keep her safe here. And safe they were.

No one was going to harm her, not if he had anything to say about it.

5

The very minute Ophelia Denton left the couple's suite, she went to the elevator.

She wasn't born yesterday. Clearly, Pam was hiding something. And if Mr. Hector told George about it, he probably let more slip than what he'd just said.

She wanted all the details.

But as she waited for the elevator, she couldn't help but look around. This was the most amazing hotel ever! The picture glass alone must have cost a fortune.

Her Mama had been a simple woman, but she'd known what her daughter wanted without Ophelia ever having to say. *Use your connections to move up in the world, baby girl*, she'd said. *This city's hard on a woman alone.*

And as the elevator doors opened, Ophelia sighed. *I wish Mama would have lived to see it.*

Here she was, in this grand hotel, with a gorgeous, rich woman who loved her.

Now, Ophelia knew she could have left the boarding house and got herself into an adjoining suite. The couple had the money.

Pam had bought her a new coat and shoes. Mr. Hector had paid for her taxis every night since he learned she got off work at two.

But it didn't feel right. Besides, she liked the girls in her boarding house. And she liked going out with them on her nights off.

Her life felt just about perfect.

She emerged into the lobby. Even though she'd been there a hundred times, the fountain in the middle of that giant room made her stop and stare. Holding her handbag with one hand and her hat with the other, she gazed at the water going up past the balcony on the second floor.

But now was not the time for gawking. "First things first," she murmured.

Ophelia went to the dining room. When she got to the Headwaiter's station, one of the maids stood there. "Welcome to the Myriad, Ma'am! What name is your table under?"

"Oh, we're not eating here 'til later. Is George Neuberg available?"

"One moment," the woman said.

After a few minutes, George showed up. "Ophie! Come on back. Want some coffee?"

"No, thanks." She followed him past men assembling meals on fine china, more men cooking, past racks of bread and rows of clean pots, back to a small office.

A real nice wooden desk full of papers, several cabinets, and a clock on the wall. George gestured to a chair in front of the desk. "Have a seat!" He sat behind the desk, leaving the door open.

"Looks like you've moving up in the world!" She took the chair he'd indicated. "You sure this is all right? Me being here?"

George laughed. "If anyone asks, I'll tell them you're interviewing." He leaned his elbows on the desk. "What can I do for you?"

Ophelia leaned back, crossing one leg over the other. "Mr. Hector showed me the flier."

George suddenly sobered. "Well, what'd you think?"

"There's something they're not telling me." And suddenly, she wondered if maybe they didn't trust her? "What did they tell you?"

George shrugged, glancing away. "That she was mixed up in some kind of Mob thing."

Ophelia felt surprised. "Oh."

"They both were. They tried to leave, but some others got involved? I don't know the details. It went bad and men were killed. So they had to get out of town," he shrugged. "I guess."

She nodded. Things like that happened here, too.

Their eyes met. "He swears she didn't kill anyone —"

"Of course she didn't. I can't see her hurting anyone!"

George turned somber. "And I guess her husband and son were killed too."

"They told me she'd lost them when we first met." But she hadn't realized it was right before they came here. "What a terrible thing to happen!"

George nodded. "And then to come to a new city? Starting fresh, I suppose. He'd been here before, just for a short time on business. But she'd never been."

"The poor dears." Ophelia felt truly sorry for them. "I wish I knew how to help."

George got real quiet. "My Pa said once that the best gauge of a man is whether he stands by his friends in trouble." Then he nodded, like he was talking to himself, really. "Seems to me that's the best way to help them."

She went over what they'd said in her mind. "They said the Feds were after them."

George's eyes widened. "Really." He stopped then, pondering a bit. "Yeah. It said that on the flier, now that I think of it."

"Well, they think she had something to do with those men dying! Anyway, they were worried we might get into trouble tonight."

George snorted. "With all the hundreds of speakeasies packed in like sardines tonight, the chance of any **we** go to being raided is nil." He gave her a wry smile and a wink. "But I'll keep you girls close and my eyes open."

Ophelia giggled. "I'll see you tonight, then."

"You bet."

She went back out and on down the street to her home, feeling real pleased and happy. George was the cat's pajamas, he really was.

He'd never once been anything but a perfect gentleman, and he never missed a chance to go out with her and her friends. The girls all liked him too. And were they envious! They couldn't get over how good-looking he was. And him going out with them seemed to make her landlady Mrs. Kilpatrick happy.

Letting the old lady and the girls think she and George were sweet on each other was a bit of a lie, but as her Mama once said, a little white lie never hurt anyone.

6

Upstairs, the couple were having a cozy evening by the fire in their parlor, listening to the sounds of the party outside.

After a while, the fire burned low, and Mr. Jackson got up to check on the dogs. There Bessie lay, raising her head when they entered. Her puppies lay sleeping around her.

Mr. Jackson said, "Ready for a walk, girl?"

Bessie delicately stepped around her new babies and trotted over, so he put her wrap and her leash on her.

"I'll keep an eye on them until you're back," Mrs. Jackson said.

Mr. Jackson and Bessie went to the elevator doors. The elevator-man smiled and waved at Bessie. "How's our little Mama tonight?"

Bessie's ears went up, and she wagged her tail.

Mr. Jackson said, "She seems well."

"And her pups?"

"They're well also." Mr. Jackson got an idea. "Would you like one?"

"Me? Naw. I've got no place to keep one. Not fair to have a dog stuck in a tenement all day."

Mr. Jackson nodded. He wouldn't have kept Bessie when they found her starving outside of the hotel, if his wife didn't love the little dog so. But the black toy poodle had certainly grown on him.

The elevator opened, and Bessie's little claws tapped on the marble floor as they went through the magnificent lobby. They passed the enormous fountain and headed towards the front doors.

The men there opened the doors for him, one on each door. "Good evening, sir!" One said.

"Good evening," he replied absentmindedly.

Hundreds of little bulbs high above the circle drive gave the place a warm inviting glow. He and Bessie moved right, towards the street, and into the crowds moving past the Myriad Hotel along Lake Shore Drive.

Warmth from the heat of the sun still radiated from the pavement, but a chill in the air spoke of a cold front coming in. Automobiles went to and fro. People clogged the darkened streets, dressed to the nines. Fireworks rose from Lake Michigan to boom high overhead. Horns, both from cars and from the hands of the passers-by, and cries of "Happy New Year!" came forth.

He looked down at little Bessie. What must she think of all this commotion?

At his gaze, her ears perked up, her tail wagging.

They walked along to the light, and went across Lake Shore Drive to the boardwalk along the rocky beach. Bessie stopped here and there to sniff, and Mr. Jackson let her. She hadn't gotten out much since her pups were born, and it seemed rude to hurry her.

"Oh, what a cute doggie!" A woman in a white fur coat and dark bobbed hair hung off the arm of her rather handsome beau, peering down at Bessie.

Mr. Jackson tipped his fedora at the pair. "Happy New Year!"

"Happy New Year!" the man said, and the two made their way along past.

The night was clear, the moon not yet up. "My dear Queen Bess," he said to the little dog. "I think this is going to be a good year."

***

Hector Jackson awoke from a sound sleep.

Bam-bam-bam

"What in the world?"

Bam-bam-bam

He got up, pulled on trousers and a robe, and made his way to the parlor door.

His wife called out from his bed, "What's wrong?"

"I'll find out."

When he opened the door, Mr. Carlo stood there in the hallway.

"Good grief, Carlo," Mr. Jackson said. "It's the middle of the night."

"Sorry to wake you at this hour," Mr. Carlo said, "but I need your help."

Mr. Jackson turned on the parlor light. "Come in."

"No need for that; I'll wait."

"Wait for what? What's going on?"

"Get dressed; I'll tell you on the way."

At first, he was going to protest. But then his curiosity got the better of him. It was one in the morning. What could possibly have happened?

Rubbing sleep from his eyes, Mr. Jackson turned off the light and returned to his room, leaving the door open. His wife lay sleeping. So he got dressed, put some water out for Bessie, then got his hat. He left a note in case his wife might wake before he returned, then moved to the open door.

Mr. Carlo still stood in the hallway.

Mr. Jackson locked the parlor door behind them. "Now what's this about?"

"Hurry," Mr. Carlo said quietly, leading him along the hall to the elevator. "A man's been murdered."

The elevator stood open and ready. As they descended, Mr. Carlo said not a word. Rather, he put a key into the wall and pressed a gold button there.

"Thank you, sir," the elevator-man said. The man was elderly, yet his back was straight, his bearing proud.

The elevator descended past the lobby, past what felt like two more floors. Then the doors opened onto a well-lit hall carpeted in rich burgundy. Mr. Carlo told the elevator-man, "Stay here." Then he grabbed Mr. Jackson's left sleeve for a second. "This way."

He let go, walking off; Mr. Jackson followed him down the hall.

"The crush at the bar must have been terrific," Mr. Carlo said. "The man just fell off his barstool about five after midnight, stone dead."

Mr. Jackson still felt foggy. "You're sure it's murder?"

Mr. Carlo chuckled. "The man's got blood all over his shirt and a bullet-hole in him. I doubt that's natural."

"Oh," Mr. Jackson said, suddenly chagrined. "And no one saw anything?"

Mr. Carlo scoffed. "The minute he hit the floor, the place emptied out." He came to a door and opened it. A thick red velvet curtain hung there, blocking the entryway. "That's why I need your help." He pushed the curtain aside and stepped through, head turned back towards Mr. Jackson as he spoke. Rather loudly. "We have to learn who did this before the cops show up!"

Utter chaos lay beyond: overturned tables and chairs atop liquor bottles and shot glasses atop streamers and confetti. Bits of dropped clothing lay here and there: a masquerade mask, a black stiletto, a feathered and bejeweled headband.

In the midst of it all stood a stern-looking man in street-clothes. "Well, sirs," Sergeant Benjamin Nestor said, "I'm afraid you're just a bit too late."

7

Apparently, the rush of people fleeing the speakeasy was so frightened and tumultuous that it attracted the notice of a passing patrolman. He ran to a telephone and called the matter in at once, fearing some ghastly scene awaited them below.

On the floor, it was just as Mr. Carlo had said: a dead man, evidently done in by just the wrong sort of shot.

Mr. Jackson said, "Do we know this fellow's name?"

Mr. Carlo shook his head.

Sergeant Nestor gestured to one of the uniformed men behind him, and they began to search the body.

"Surely someone stayed behind," Mr. Jackson said. "Not even the bartender?"

A waiter came out from the back. "He's in here," the young man said. "Says he don't feel good."

One of the uniformed police stood. "A pack of cigarettes, a memo book, seventeen bucks and a business card." He scrutinized the card. "A.B. Nelson: Small Repair Our Specialty." He shrugged. "The address is on the East Side."

"Hand over the card and the book," Sergeant Nestor said. "The rest in his belongings file."

The memo book looked brand-new. "A phone number." Sergeant Nestor flipped the page. "And another number." He showed that to Mr. Carlo.

Mr. Carlo turned red. "Tonight's code to enter here."

Sergeant Nestor snorted. "What you serve people is between you and the Feds. What I care about is who killed this man and why." He looked wearily around the room. "We're going to be here all night." For the first time, he seemed to notice Mr. Jackson. "What are **you** doing here?"

"Dragged out of bed by Mr. Carlo," Mr. Jackson grumbled. "I'd much rather be upstairs." He put his hat back on. "So if you don't mind ..."

Mr. Carlo planted his fists on his hips. "Now you wait just a minute —"

Sergeant Nestor held up a hand. "Before you go, I'd like to know two things. First, where you were at midnight —"

"That's easy," Mr. Jackson said. "In bed asleep next to my wife."

"— and second, what you see here."

That last bit threw Mr. Jackson for a loop. "What?"

"I've come to realize that you see things in a different way." Sergeant Nestor grinned. "So, sir, if you wouldn't mind?"

Mr. Jackson had helped the sergeant in a couple of cases before, but that didn't mean he was some sort of expert! He rubbed his eyes and let out a yawn. "Where's the lighter?"

Mr. Carlo said, "Huh?"

"My wife's a smoker. The man had cigarettes in his pocket. Where's his lighter?"

Sergeant Nestor called over to his men. "You find a cigarette lighter anywhere?"

They shook their heads.

Sergeant Nestor said, "That's a start."

Mr. Jackson felt out of sorts. "You're going to have a hard time learning much without any witnesses."

"Okay, wise guy," Sergeant Nestor grumbled. "See anything else?"

At that, Mr. Jackson really looked at the room. The man on the floor, where the shot must have happened. "Whoever did it was right next to him. They had to have gotten blood on themselves, or at least powder. And a gunshot's far from quiet." He yawned, feeling weary. "Yet no one even noticed until the dead man fell on the **floor**?" His voice echoed in the room. "How many people were **in** here?"

Sergeant Nestor nodded. "Well, sir, we have at least one witness. Let's go talk to him."

***

The bartender, Mr. Ralph D'Angelo, was a young man, not yet thirty. He sat in the back room pale and sweaty, like he was about to be sick. "It was people everywhere. The man just had his head on his arms, leaned over like he was tired. I woulda asked him to go take a table so others could order but there was too many asking all at once. Then all of a sudden he wasn't there. First I knew anything was wrong was they started screaming." He bent over, elbows on his knees. "Never saw a dead person before, not like that."

Sergeant Nestor put his hand on the man's shoulder. "It's okay, son, just tell us what you can."

"I've been here six years and never saw so many in here. They couldn't dance, could barely pass by. There was a band on stage, and some of the flappers got up to sittin' on the stage 'cause there was no seats."

"So what happened at midnight?"

"Just like I said. Right before, everyone wanted a drink all at once. I was the only one there." He put his head in his hands. "I started just handing out bottles —"

Mr. Carlo said, "What?"

"I kept note for their tabs. Most of 'em was regulars."

"Well, that'll help," Sergeant Nestor said.

Mr. Carlo's eyes narrowed. "If you think I'm giving out my customer list, you —"

Sergeant Nestor held up a thick hand. "You can cooperate, or I can close this hotel down."

The two men scowled at each other for a moment, then Mr. Carlo's face fell. "Very well. But I'll not have anyone dragged in for questioning. You hear?"

"We'll be discreet." The sergeant turned to Mr. D'Angelo. "So you're handing out bottles. What then?"

The man let out a short laugh. "Midnight was all corks at once, and the band, and the singing, and the horns. A cannon could have gone off and no one would've hardly noticed!" He stopped then, pensive. "That man should never have died there." He sat quietly for a moment, then looked up at the sergeant. "I didn't even know it'd happened til the screaming."

Sergeant Nestor pulled up a chair beside the man. "Then what happened?"

"Everyone's looking down with their hands on their faces. Then people started pushing to get out. I'm surprised no one else is dead: it was a stampede. Women got shoved down crying, men were climbing over each other —" He stopped then, eyes far away. "That was the worst of it."

"That explains the blood on the floor on the way in," Sergeant Nestor said.

Mr. Jackson stared at him, appalled. "What?"

Sergeant Nestor nodded, then turned to one of his men who stood in the doorway. "Check with the hospitals around here. Someone's bound to have turned up. But don't scare them. They're more likely to be a witness than the killer."

He turned to Mr. Jackson. "What do you think?"

The answer came to him at once. "My guess is that the killer's a woman. She likely left shortly before midnight."

Mr. Carlo said, "A woman?"

Mr. Jackson felt amused. "Raise your arm and hold it in front of you." When Mr. Carlo did so, Mr. Jackson quickly moved towards him, intending to stand close enough that they were touching.

But before that came close to happening, Mr. Carlo flinched away, offended. "What are you on about?"

Sergeant Nestor was nodding.

"You see?" Mr. Jackson raised a finger. "A man would never let another man get so close as to do this to him, even one he'd known for some time, and presumably trusted with his livelihood."

"Oh," said Mr. Carlo, surprise on his face. "I see."

" It's likely women stood on both sides of him."

"So," Sergeant Nestor said to the bartender, who if anything, looked more unwell. "What woman stood on the man's left side?"

"I swear to you," the man said, shaking his head, "I don't recall."

8

The three others drew aside.

"He's clearly lying," Mr. Carlo whispered. "I'll get it out of him."

"No, no, no," said the sergeant, just as softly. "He's not the one we're after. Besides, if he has some connection with the woman and he's harmed — and she learns of it — she'll only flee." He tapped his chin. "No, I think other forms of persuasion might be better served." He turned to the bartender. "You're free to go. sir." He handed the man a card. "If you recall anything else, be sure to phone me."

"Yes, sir." Mr. D'Angelo stood, somewhat unsteadily, and began collecting his coat and hat.

Sergeant Nestor called to one of his men. "See this fellow home, will you? He doesn't look at all well. Make sure he gets into bed safe. He's had a difficult evening." As the officer and Mr. D'Angelo left, Sergeant Nestor said to Mr. Carlo, "Now we'll learn where he lives, and perhaps even who else lives with him. Now for your tab list, sir."

Mr. Carlo scowled.

Mr. Jackson said, "Anything else?"

Sergeant Nestor snorted. "Can you think of anything else?"

Curse my active brain, Mr. Jackson thought. Somehow, the one waiter who'd stayed around had disappeared. "Where are the **other** waiters? The bouncers? The band? There are a whole line of people who should be here, if only to get paid." He turned to Mr. Carlo. "Another list for the sergeant."

"Good man," Sergeant Nestor said. "I'd entirely forgotten about the bouncers. You go up to your wife; I'll stop by tomorrow sometime. After lunch, perhaps?"

"Very well," Mr. Jackson said. "Good night."

As Mr. Jackson left, the sergeant shouted, "I want this place dusted for prints. I don't care if it takes all night."

So Mr. Jackson trudged back to his rooms to the groans and grumbles of the other officers and got into bed without his wife even stirring. Though he'd been afraid of the matter keeping him awake all night, he fell asleep at once.

***

When Mrs. Jackson woke, her Mr. Jackson lay in bed with his clothes still on, his jacket, hat, and shoes in a pile beside the bed. "You poor dear," she murmured, smoothing his brow. "What did that Mr. Carlo have you up to this time?" She'd recognized the man's voice before she drifted off, but even that hadn't kept her awake to make sure all was well.

I must be feeling safe here, she thought.

She tried to make him more comfortable, loosening his collar and removing his belt before covering him up with a kiss on the forehead. Then a check on Bessie and the puppies. Bessie was ready to go out, dancing around.

"Shh," Mrs. Jackson said as she put Bessie's wrap and leash on.

She brought Bessie into her bathroom to freshen up. A quick change into a long navy blue day dress of fine wool, thick stockings and stout shoes, a long wool jacket, cloche hat, and gloves, and they were out of the door.

The sun was up: it was past time to meet Monsieur.

As she waited for the elevator, she had a tickle in her throat, which turned into a cough.

When she emerged from the elevator, she unhooked Bessie's leash and stood by the elevator door smoking as Bessie made her rounds nearby. The day was cold and overcast, the sun a pale ball in the sky.

She finished the cigarette before moving further. Monsieur didn't like her smoking around the plants; apparently the tobacco was harmful to them.

The young Chef stood, dusting off his hands as she approached. With him were several other young men around large tall carts holding baskets full of long fat carrots. He nodded to her, then dismissed the men, who took the carts and moved past her back the way she came. "Good morning," Monsieur said.

Mrs. Jackson said, "Did your New Year's go well?"

He shrugged. "I don't care for drink, and I was here at the crack of dawn." He chuckled. "I slept soundly enough. Better than your husband, from what I hear."

"Oh?"

Monsieur blinked. "Apparently, a man was killed downstairs. I presumed that Mr. Carlo called in your husband. The staff were all speaking of it when I went to check on the bakery."

"Yes, he went out," Mrs. Jackson said, "late last night. But this is the first I've heard of anyone killed."

"Forgive me," Monsieur said. "I'm sure your husband can tell you more of it."

Monsieur set her to covering the area where the carrots had been with a thick layer of compost. This lay in a wheelbarrow with a large scoop in it.

Yet breakfast-time beckoned: he needed to return to the kitchens.

So she poured the material, which looked and smelled of rich earth, to cover the entire bare space, with Bessie running around at every movement. Then she smoothed it with the back of the large metal scoop. "This will teach me not to be late," she told Bessie, only half grumbling.

By the time Mrs. Jackson and Bessie returned to their rooms, Mr. Jackson had a full breakfast set upon the parlor table! "I thought you might feel hungry."

When Mrs. Jackson undid the wrap, Bessie ran to her puppies, her little claws clacking on the tile of Mr. Jackson's bathroom.

Mrs. Jackson washed her hands, then put her coat, hat, and gloves on the sofa, sitting in an armchair beside him. "That was quite thoughtful of you," she said. "And how are our little guests?"

He smiled warmly at her, passing her a dish of scrambled eggs. "They seem well. One opened his eyes!"

She chuckled at the news and laid her napkin on her lap. "How our babies have grown."

Mr. Jackson nodded, mouth full.

She loved the sight of his dark, dark skin upon the fine white china. "Monsieur spoke of a commotion downstairs. A murder?"

Mr. Jackson chewed, swallowed. "Yes, unfortunately. In the speakeasy."

She felt intrigued. "So there **is** one down there!"

He chuckled. "It's rather grand, actually. Although not nearly as large as the one Miss Denton performs in."

"She'll be glad to hear it."

"Mr. Carlo wasn't too pleased that the sergeant was there already," Mr. Jackson said, "but I suppose it couldn't be helped. He said he might stop by this afternoon."

"Mr. Carlo?"

"No, forgive me. The sergeant." Mr. Jackson frowned slightly. "I wonder why?"

Mrs. Jackson shrugged. "I'd be surprised if he thought **we** might help."

"Well, he might need the help, to be honest. The place was an utter disaster! Even the tables were overturned. It sounded as though it was much too crowded, then in the fright of discovering the body, the entire lot rushed out at once." Mr. Jackson shook his head. "It must have been a madhouse."

"Hmm." Mrs. Jackson took a sip of her tea. "More likely the fright was at the prospect of being found by the police, not only at a speakeasy, but with a dead body to boot."

Mr. Jackson chuckled.

She picked up a half-slice of toast. "I'm just glad he called you down, not me."

"For shame! Wishing your poor husband dragged from his bed to gaze upon a murder scene?" He poked her side.

She let out a yelp, and began giggling.

Bessie padded out, giving them a disapproving eye.

"Oh, dear. We'll mind our manners," Mrs. Jackson said to Bessie. Then she said to Mr. Jackson, "I suppose we should be quieter, if only for the sake of the puppies." But then a giggle came from her once more.

Bessie let out a "ruff" and returned to her pups.

Mr. Jackson said, "You know you've misbehaved when your dog comes out to reprove you!"

She put the remains of their breakfast on a saucer beside Bessie and refilled the little dog's water bowl.

Outside the French doors lay dreary and gray, and Mrs. Jackson felt glad to stay in their rooms. Who would want to go out on New Year's Day if they didn't have to?

They lit the fire and sat on the sofa, he reading the news, she a copy of *The Great Impersonation*. Duchess Cordelia had recommended the book, describing it as a most exciting tale. And once Mrs. Jackson got past the horrible vile fellow at the start of it, the tale was proving to be quite interesting thus far.

From time to time, Bessie came out to snuggle on the floor beside one of them. Then she'd hear a slight sound from her children, it seemed, because her ears would perk up, and she'd trot back over to them.

Mid-morning, Mrs. Jackson put Bessie's wrap on and called down for someone to come walk her. Soon one of the veterinarian's many sons knocked on the parlor door.

Bessie immediately ran to him. A bright-eyed boy of ten, he smiled shyly at them, clipped Bessie's leash on, and went right off down the hall as Bessie danced about alongside him.

Mrs. Jackson smiled after them, feeling warmed. "They do love our little dog so."

Mr. Jackson said from the sofa, "How about we have luncheon downstairs?"

Mrs. Jackson closed the door. "That would be splendid!" Then she laughed, going to him. "Pet says I'm terribly old-fashioned when I say that."

"What?"

She sat on the sofa beside him. "Splendid."

He chuckled. "It's a perfectly respectable word."

She suddenly felt somber. The sofa's velvet felt soft yet a touch bristly. "But they don't say it here. It marks me as an outsider."

She felt his hand in her hair, his kiss on her forehead. He spoke softly. "Chicago is full of outsiders, dear girl. No one will care about one or two more."

She buried her face in his chest, listening to the slow beat of his heart. He wasn't afraid in the slightest. But when would the fear of being found, captured, brought back ... when would it ever leave her?

9

Mr. Jackson held his wife in his arms. The prospect of being discovered still terrified her. "Do you want to stay somewhere else?"

He knew before she laughed he'd said the right thing.

"And leave our friends? Of course not. I like it here! Besides, the puppies are much too young to travel."

He shrugged. "Then stop this worry." He kissed her curly black hair, her light brown forehead, lifted her chin to gaze into those beautiful blue eyes. He kept his voice light. "You hear me? I forbid it. Worry when it's time to. But before then, it does nothing but upset the digestion."

She gave him a broad smile in return. "You are ever so sensible, as always." Then she turned round, leaned her back upon him. "Now tell me about this murder."

Mr. Jackson burst out laughing. "Is it the gory detail which intrigues you, or the puzzle of it all?"

"The puzzle, of course," she said, as if this were obvious. "Tell me everything."

So he related what he'd seen: the empty underground speakeasy in shambles, the man lying dead with a gunshot in his side.

"You say there were no witnesses?"

"Well, the bartender stayed at his post," Mr. Jackson wondered why, when most everyone else had not. "And one waiter, but he slipped out soon after. I think his concern was the state the other man was in."

"Not everyone has seen sudden death," his wife said soberly. "It changes you."

From what he'd gathered, she'd seen her fair share. But then she'd been an actual investigator, long before they were ever married. "I suppose it does."

"Well, this is a situation," she said somberly. "One dead man and no witnesses. I suppose old Nestor had his men up all night dusting for prints."

Mr. Jackson laughed in surprise. "Exactly right!"

She shrugged. "It's what I'd do in his place."

"You'd make a fair cop," he said. "Ever consider it?"

She turned to face him, and he immediately realized his error. Her people didn't exactly have a good relationship with the police, and he should have recalled it. But her face was amused, not angry. "Now why in the world would I **ever** want to do that?" She turned around to snuggle her back into his side once more. "Particularly with such a nice warm spot here."

"You silly girl," he said fondly. Then he recalled the date. "I forgot to say it: Happy New Year."

She took his arms in turn, wrapping each one of them round her. "Happy New Year to you too, my love."

***

After Bessie returned from her walk, it was time for luncheon. So the couple tidied the area around Bessie and her pups (so as not to cause the maids too much trouble), put the "Please clean room now" sign on, and left for their meal.

Lee Francis, the head clerk, now stood at the front desk. "Good to see you!"

Mr. Jackson said, "Happy New Year, sir." He extended a hand for the fellow to shake. "I feared you might not be here today."

"Just filling in: my clerk had to leave just now." He rubbed the back of his neck. "Afternoon shift starts soon, then I'll be on my way." His tone turned bright. "And how's our little puppy doing?"

Mr. Francis and his wife had already chosen out one of Bessie's puppies for their new son. Mr. Jackson smiled. "He opened his eyes today!"

"Already? That sounds like a good sign."

"Indeed it is."

"Well, I won't keep you. Enjoy your luncheon."

George beamed when he saw them. "Happy New Year to you both!"

Mrs. Jackson took George's hand. "Dear George. I hope those young ladies didn't keep you up too late."

He chuckled. "No later than I've kept myself in the past. No, I saw them safe in their house by three."

Mr. Jackson thought it amusing how his wife's eyebrows raised. "Three?"

George gave her a bemused smile. "I didn't need to be here until noon. So plenty of time for napping."

As Headwaiter, most of George's work seemed to be greeting important guests (of which there were many) and making sure the front room was properly staffed. He'd also made some improvements to the seating flow and to the decor. He'd also moved to an apartment around the corner.

George escorted the couple to a table. "Have any plans for today?"

"Not really," Mrs. Jackson said. "We'll probably stay in for dinner. But you're welcome to stop by, if you like."

"I may just. One of my waiters is running late, but he should be here shortly." He glanced back at the door, where a well-dressed pair stood waiting, then winked at them. "Toodle-ooo!"

The couple laughed softly as he left.

Maria, the Myriad's Head Maid, a stout woman with dark curls, approached, holding a notepad and pencil. "The usual?"

Mr. Jackson said. "The Chef's Special for us both." They'd gotten the Chef's Special menu ever since Monsieur arrived here, and the young man had yet to disappoint. "Coffee for me, lots of heavy cream, but no sugar, and —"

"Tea for the missus. Yes, sir, right away." She headed off to the next table.

His wife laughed. "She's got us pegged."

The meal was — in a word — delicious. A thick potato soup, dotted with bits of bacon and rosemary. Hot sugar-cured ham with a cider sauce topped by preserved figs. Small wedges of mild cheddar, made by Monsieur here in the Hotel. Dill-pickled cucumbers, thinly sliced. A salad of new greens with a lemony sauce.

They lingered over their meal. The warm glow of the room, the music from the piano ... it soothed him.

"I wonder where Duchess Cordelia is," said his wife. "Do you see her?"

"I don't," he said. "Perhaps she took her luncheon in her rooms."

"That must be it."

He patted her hand. "I'm sure she's fine. Not everyone cares to stir from their rooms on the holiday."

"True." His wife returned to her tea.

Just then, Mr. Carlo entered the dining room. George and all the waiters came subtly to attention, their faces taking carefully neutral smiles. Mr. Jackson laughed.

His wife peered at him. "What is it?"

He gestured with his chin. "Carlo's here."

"Heh," said his wife.

George gestured their way, and Mr. Carlo made a beeline for their table.

His wife said, "I wonder what he wants."

As usual, Mr. Carlo had an impatient air. "Well?"

"Good day to you too," his wife said.

Mr. Jackson chuckled. "Well, what?"

"The sergeant's here to see you. He said he told you he'd be by after luncheon."

Mr. Jackson checked his watch: 1:40. "I didn't think he'd brown-bag it and sit at our doorstep."

That even made Mr. Carlo laugh. "Yeah, he's sure keen about this one. Probably because it's in my hotel."

The sergeant never seemed to get along with those of money, and particularly seemed to have it in for Mr. Carlo. "Oh, very well," Mr. Jackson said. He glanced at his wife, who seemed bemused by the whole affair. "I think we're done here, don't you?"

She beamed at him, and for an instant he thought he might never breathe.

But then she rose. "Come on then," she said. "Can't keep the old guy waiting."

10

But Sergeant Nestor wasn't at the desk. The clerk solved that mystery. "He's gone up to wait for you," the young man said.

"Thank you." Taking Mr. Jackson's offered arm, she followed Mr. Carlo to the elevator, watching with amusement as the man fidgeted, tapping his foot. She felt a bit sorry for the elevator's young operator, who certainly couldn't make the contraption go any faster!

She ventured, "I hope your family's well?"

She'd had chance to meet his wife and daughter in the spring, when they first arrived here at the Myriad. She hoped the mention of loved ones might settle the man.

But he gave her a sharp glance. "Margaret's taken ill. Her husband's out of town, so Maisy's home with her."

"Nothing serious, I hope?" The terrible flu that had ravaged the country recently seemed to have subsided somewhat. And Chicago had fared better than most.

He shrugged, suddenly downcast. "The doctor doesn't think so. But I'll not take any chances."

Margaret was his only child; Mrs. Jackson understood his sentiments. "I'll light a candle for her healing, sir."

Relief and gratitude crossed the man's face. "That's very kind of you."

The elevator door opened, and they went along the hallways to the couple's rooms. But the sergeant wasn't in the hall.

Mr. Jackson took out the key, but the door opened on its own. "What's this?"

"Perhaps the maid's here," said Mr. Carlo. "Why she's here without her cart, I have no idea." Then he called, "Lela?"

Hearing no answer, the three moved into the parlor, closing the door behind them.

A voice came from Mr. Jackson's bathroom. "Oh, my — aren't you a handsome set."

They found the sergeant in a squat position, admiring Bessie's puppies. He glanced up at them. "Your little stray's done quite well for herself here."

Mr. Carlo looked horrified. "You have a litter of **puppies**? In my **hotel**?"

Mrs. Jackson felt quite amused.

Her Mr. Jackson, on the other hand, sounded positively exasperated. "What are you doing in my bathroom? How did you get in here?"

Sergeant Nestor shrugged, bouncing up to a standing position. "I had the maid let me in."

She seldom saw her Mr. Jackson at a loss for words. But then he recovered himself, glancing at Mr. Carlo and the sergeant. "Would either of you like one?"

To Mrs. Jackson's surprise, Sergeant Nestor seemed to seriously consider the offer. "My oldest son might like that dark brown one. I'll ask him!" He gestured to the door. "In the meantime, let's discuss the case at hand."

At that, Mr. Carlo seemed to recover from his sudden shock. So they all went to the parlor, sitting around the rosewood table.

Mrs. Jackson thought it best to be polite. "Care for some tea?" But her offers were declined, so she sat with the rest. "How might we possibly help you?"

Sergeant Nestor hesitated.

"I don't want this in the press," Mr. Carlo said.

At the exact same time, Sergeant Nestor said, "No one will talk to my men."

They looked at each other.

Mr. Jackson put his arm around her shoulders. "I won't have my wife down there."

She felt amused at this. "But if you need our help, whatever we can do," she looked up at Mr. Jackson, "we'd be happy to."

Sergeant Nestor put his elbows firmly on the table. "We found lipstick upon the man's collar and cheeks —"

Mr. and Mrs. Jackson nodded, then glanced at each other in surprise.

"— this confirms that a woman might be involved."

Mr. Carlo exclaimed. "The place was packed with women. But a murderess?"

Mrs. Jackson scoffed. "I assure you, sir, a woman can have as black a heart as any man."

All three men gaped at her. Then Mr. Jackson drew back, hand to his chin, gazing at the table.

"Well," Sergeant Nestor said, "three shades of lip color were found on the body —"

"That makes things more interesting," said Mrs. Jackson.

"Yes, " Sergeant Nestor said, perhaps irritated by her interruptions. "So at least three possible suspects."

Mr. Jackson stirred. "Did your fingerprint dusting bear any fruit?"

Sergeant Nestor let out an ironic, amused chuckle. "Too much fruit. Hundreds of partial prints. It's going to take a whole team to sort this one out."

"Hmm," said Mrs. Jackson. "So that might not be so helpful."

"It'll help narrow things down," said the sergeant, "particularly those prints near the dead man." He leaned back. "Who we've not yet identified, by the way."

Mr. Carlo said, "So no one knew the man's **name**?"

The sergeant shrugged. "If they do, no one's saying. No one's answering the number on the business card, but I don't expect a shop would have anyone in on a holiday. My men have questioned everyone scheduled to work that night, including the band members, but they all claim they never saw a thing."

Mr. Carlo stood. "I'll get it out of them."

Sergeant Nestor held up a hand. "Now, now, sir: you simply can't proceed like this! Just leave it to me. I don't want anyone giving a name out of fear — in my experience, that only makes this take all the longer." He stood, facing the man. "Encourage them to cooperate with us. But no strong-arm tactics, or I'll bar you from the investigation. Is that clear?"

Mr. Carlo scowled, then nodded.

Sergeant Nestor sat. "I'll take some of that tea, if you've got it handy."

They didn't actually have it handy, but Mrs. Jackson called to have some sent up. When she returned to the room, Mr. Carlo was seated again.

Sergeant Nestor was saying, "— remembers a man buying one the other day, and —"

So she said, "Buying what?"

The sergeant glanced up. "The memo book. In his pocket. It was new." He looked over at Mr. Jackson. "What all did you tell her?"

Mr. Jackson shrugged. "We really haven't discussed it that much."

Mrs. Jackson didn't want to contradict him. Besides, she was interested in what the sergeant had to say. So she made her way back to her chair.

Sergeant Nestor sighed. "Very well." And with that, he went into a story of panicked drunken people pouring out onto the streets around the hotel just after midnight, with an equally panicked young officer phoning him at home. Coming upon the room, and Mr. Carlo and Mr. Jackson entering. The scene, the position of the body. "I suppose that brings you up to speed on this one."

She considered the matter. "So he only had the notebook in his pocket? No wallet?"

"Nope. A pack of cigarettes, seventeen bucks and a business card to a repair shop."

"And he was shot in his side. Just the once?"

"Right," said the sergeant. "Small caliber."

She'd figured that, since they never mentioned an exit wound, nor anyone else being injured by it. "So it's still in there. I suppose that could help."

"It will," Sergeant Nestor said. "The gun was pressed to his left side, fired through the man's vest. The bullet appears to have gone straight through his heart."

Mrs. Jackson remembered the night her husband died. His face. The bullet-hole over his heart. His last words to her.

"Heh," Mr. Jackson said. "Personal indeed."

Mr. Carlo nodded.

Mrs. Jackson took a deep breath, trying to make her voice bright. "And the perfect timing! Right when the noise was so great you could have probably screamed and not been heard."

Sergeant Nestor said, "From the reports so far and the man's face, I don't think he even knew what hit him." He seemed to consider this for a moment. "Strange, to one moment be alive, the next dead." Then he shrugged. "Not the worst way to go, I suppose."

Mrs. Jackson didn't know what to say, and neither did anyone else, it seemed, for the next sound was the parlor door-bell. "Tea's here." She went to the door.

The maid poured tea all round, a bit awed to have Mr. Carlo there, it seemed, but soon she was out and the parlor door shut.

Something still bothered Mrs. Jackson, though. "So no one knew the man was dead until he fell?"

"Apparently not," Mr. Jackson said.

"A dead man doesn't sit on a barstool without help," Mrs. Jackson said. "So the murderer was had to have positioned him afterwards. Perhaps folding the man's arms on the bar, resting his head upon them." She demonstrated. "Like so. Otherwise, the dead man would just slump over. Right?"

Sergeant Nestor nodded. "The bartender said he saw the man positioned that way."

Mr. Jackson said, "Someone had to have seen who did that for him."

Mrs. Jackson said, "Right. But it's something anyone might do for a friend who's passed out, or very drunk, or feeling unwell. So —"

"So no one thought anything of it," Mr. Jackson said.

Mrs. Jackson nodded. "Exactly."

Mr. Jackson peered at her, face filled with concern. "Wait. Didn't the bartender say he saw the man hunched over the bar **before** twelve?"

Mr. Carlo's face froze in surprise. "He did!"

"Heh," Sergeant Nestor said to Mr. Jackson. "Good call. I'll have the autopsy-man look for sedatives."

Sedate a man, **then** shoot him?

Sergeant Nestor and Mr. Carlo exchanged a glance. Mr. Carlo said, "Now you see why I keep them here."

The sergeant raised his eyebrows.

Mrs. Jackson thought it an odd choice of words. But so far the man had refused any payment for their lodgings. "In any case, he — or she, most likely — drugs the man, gets him settled," she tried to picture the scene, "then at the stroke of twelve, shoots the man and makes for the door. Did your doormen see any women leave right before the commotion?"

"The doormen won't be in until tonight," Mr. Carlo said. "But it's likely there were dozens of women going in and out: to the toilets, to smoke, both alone and with their men."

She persisted. "But any acting strangely, or someone who didn't come back in."

"We could ask, of course," Sergeant Nestor said. "But I think someone calm enough to not only plan but actually do this might have the presence of mind to act casually on the way out." His eyes narrowed. "That is, if they even left before the panic."

Mr. Carlo put down his tea. "Why would anyone knowing a stampede was about to occur stay around?"

Mr. Jackson had a strange look upon his face. "Are there any other ways out of the room? Other than the one hallway and the way we came in?"

This gave Mrs. Jackson a shock. "There were two ways out?"

"Of course," said Mr. Carlo. "But you can't take the elevator without a key."

Sergeant Nestor said, "Who else had the key?"

11

It turned out a great many people had the key, including the bartender. "The first to 'discover' a body is the most likely suspect," Sergeant Nestor said, "so I made a call. Our friend has a prison record."

"Well," Mr. Carlo said, annoyed perhaps at the play for suspense, "what did the man **do**?"

"Robbed a grocery at gunpoint," the sergeant said, "eight years ago. The man said it was to feed his family, so they gave him a light sentence. But I have the fellow in for questioning right now." He tapped his chin. "I think he knows more than he's saying."

Mr. Jackson said, "It's interesting that the man had his own way out, yet never took it."

"Which is one of several reasons I don't think he did it," Sergeant Nestor said. "But I think he may know who did. Or at the very least, know who this dead fellow really is."

Mrs. Jackson nodded. It made sense. "Have you located any of the other customers?"

Before Sergeant Nestor might speak, Mr. Jackson said, "No. It's not the customers we need now. Who we need to talk with at once was that old elevator-man."

"Already done," Sergeant Nestor said. "He doesn't recall anyone coming up that elevator most of the evening, well," he gestured at Mr. Jackson and Mr. Carlo, "except you two."

Strange, Mrs. Jackson thought. "Most of the evening?"

The sergeant turned to Mr. Carlo. "Later that night, one of your cleaning women came on, a pretty brown-haired girl. He says it was perhaps three. He didn't recognize her, and it surprised him as they're supposed to take the service elevator —"

"So there's yet a third way out," said Mr. Jackson.

Mr. Carlo nodded.

Mrs. Jackson said, "He didn't recognize her?"

Sergeant Nestor gave her a quick glance. "She claimed she was new, and had been given the wrong key. You need one for the service elevator, you see. But she had the key, and wore the uniform, and had a name-tag, even, just like the rest."

Mr. Jackson said, "What name was on the tag?"

"Maria."

Mrs. Jackson said, "I know Maria! She's Head Maid, works days. That can't have been her: the woman's at least forty."

Sergeant Nestor raised an eyebrow. "I suppose we'd best talk to this elevator-man again."

While Sergeant Nestor was on the telephone with the elevator-man (who was at home), Mr. Carlo called Maria upstairs to the couple's rooms.

"My name-tag went missing three days back," Maria said. "They're making a new one for me. Not that I much need it: I've been here since this place opened."

"So you have," said Mr. Carlo. "Now, keep it to yourself that I called you up here, will you?"

She gave the room a quick glance. "It's about that fellow downstairs dead, isn't it."

"It is," Mr. Carlo said. "And the fewer who know of it, the better."

"Right," she said firmly. "No one will hear of this from me!"

"Very good," Mr. Carlo said. "You may go."

Once Maria had left, Sergeant Nestor turned to them. "I got a fair description of her from the elevator-man on duty last night: dark brown hair, blue eyes. He said she came to his shoulder, and the man's —"

"Almost as tall as me," Mr. Jackson said.

Mrs. Jackson nodded. "Did you find that bullet yet?"

Sergeant Nestor shrugged. "Autopsy won't be until tomorrow at the earliest. The holiday?"

She'd forgotten. "Right." For a moment, she felt foolish. Then she moved around to sit on the other side of Mr. Jackson. "In any case, sitting on barstools, her arm round him, he probably put his arm round her," she demonstrated with her hand, as if holding a gun at the level of her lower chest, right below her breasts. "She'd have to hold the gun left-handed. So she's either left-handed, or —"

"Fairly well-practiced shooting with either hand," her Mr. Jackson said.

"Yes," she said. "And there's something else: I'm too short to be the killer. I'd have to angle up to be sure to kill him." She shuddered, recalling the heat of a muzzle flash and the skimpy little dresses young women wore to nightclubs here. "I wouldn't want to try doing that with bare arms! In any case, for that to go straight into his heart, she'd **have** to be taller than me, by a good bit."

Sergeant Nestor gazed at her. "You'd make a fair cop."

She scoffed at the very suggestion. "Not me. I'm only helping you because you helped me in the past." She smiled to herself. "And I do love a good puzzle."

The parlor door-bell rang, and Mr. Jackson went to get it.

"Hello," George said, and he sounded surprised. "We having a party?"

12

"You gotta be kidding me," George said. The police officer and Mr. Carlo had gone, and he sat in the parlor with Hector and Pam.

"I assure you, we're not," Hector said. "We've helped with this sort of thing before. Remember when you had the bad lemon-cake?"

George grimaced, his stomach clenching at the memory. "How could I forget?" He'd come close to dying that time.

"And the trouble with the Head Valet?"

He felt astonished. "You helped with that, too?"

Pam gave him a smile that made him feel very young, and more than a bit foolish. "We most certainly did."

How could they possibly have been involved with all this without him knowing? George peered at them, bewildered. "And that officer wants you to help once more. With a murder?" He had a sudden fear for them. "Isn't that dangerous?"

Hector sighed. "I suppose it could be. But we owe them both a debt of gratitude: they're the ones helping to keep our secret. And if they need our help, small as it might be, then we're glad to be of service." He leaned forward, his face suddenly serious. "But you mustn't tell anyone. I don't think Mr. Carlo was very happy for you to see the four of us here together."

George nodded. "My job depends on good publicity. And I wouldn't like our young Chef being linked to something like this."

Hector nodded.

Pam looked absolutely appalled at the notion. "Certainly not!"

Which was odd. He wasn't aware she even knew the little fellow. "What can I do to help?"

"Nothing at present," Hector said. "Today, as I've been reminded, is a holiday." He stretched. "And I plan to enjoy it."

***

Mr. Jackson meant what he said, but of course life got in the way.

George became bored with sitting and left. Then his wife said, "There's something troubling me."

This sparked his attention at once. "Oh?"

"Mr. Carlo." She hesitated. "I don't like how he speaks of us."

He tried to recall what Mr. Carlo might have said to offend, but failed to. "I don't understand."

"Remember when he and the sergeant were here? He said, 'you see why I keep them here'?" She stopped, took a deep breath. "And you said 'Mr. Carlo has been picking up the tab'. Do you see? My concern is —"

He'd been staring at her, mouth open. "You have a remarkable memory for detail."

She scoffed. "So they tell me. What I'm saying is —"

"You think he thinks he's bought us."

A small laugh burst from her. "Yeah, and he's in the process of making his own little empire." She shook her head bitterly. "I just got out of one Mob family — I won't be dragged into another!"

Mr. Jackson felt floored. "Forgive me." She was absolutely right. What could he say? "Letting him cover the tab was easy, and ... convenient, and ... I'm sorry to have caused you this worry." They were in a dilemma, but one he thought would be easy to remedy. "I'll take care of this at once."

She shrugged, her manner relaxed. "There's really nothing to forgive."

"His demeanor when he woke me last night — well, I suppose it was this morning, really — it now makes sense. If I hadn't been half asleep when I answered the door, I would've told him to buzz off"

"Well, it may be a good thing you didn't," his wife said. "The evening might not have gone nearly so well."

"True." If Carlo had thought his generosity meant he might call on their service at any hour of the day or night, then balking at what he considered a reasonable request could have meant the end of their stay here. And he had nowhere in particular planned for them to go.

He'd been lax, lulled into a state of complacency. "I've just let myself become too comfortable." He leaned forward. "It won't happen again."

She gave him a warm smile. "This place is altogether too lovely." She laughed softly. "It's meant for relaxation and comfort, not mysteries and intrigue." She leaned over to kiss his cheek, then winked at him. "I'm going on the balcony for a smoke."

Bessie came out to put her little paws on his leg, so on went the little dog's wrap and leash, and off they went.

When they got down to the lobby, they met the veterinarian coming out from his offices down the hall. "Afternoon," the man said. "Off for a stroll?"

The three continued towards the lobby. "We are," Mr. Jackson said. "Looks like a fine day."

The veterinarian stopped. "Oh. No, don't take her out there: it's well below freezing! We've been walking them in the gardens." He gestured to Bessie's feet. "Much too cold for their little paws when they're inside all day."

"I didn't consider that." Mr. Jackson felt somewhat embarrassed.

The veterinarian smiled at him. "Don't mention it. Glad I caught you." He hurried out the front door, turning his collar up as he went.

"Well, Miss Bessie," Mr. Jackson said quietly, "I suppose we'll just have to take a tour of the gardens."

The beveled glass door to the gardens lay underneath the wide staircase, down a wide hallway. Once inside, a lush, grand garden stretched before them. Bessie pulled off the walkway towards the dirt, where she made the most of the opportunity beside a small tree.

That done, they began their stroll along the pathway of grayish-brown brick. The trees, the bushes, the flowers. A moist smell of dirt, a sound of running water. All was quiet, serene, as they strolled along the winding path. The vaulted, glassed-in roof reminded him of his childhood home, and he wondered how his sister fared.

She'd received his letters, sending a long reply to a P.O. Box address in an entirely different part of the country. As always, she wrote of home, family, and children — particularly her newest son — and the funny little things they did.

"Mama was quite pleasantly surprised to hear of your marriage! But I've told no one else, and I've said nothing at all about your wife. Everyone believes you're off on one of your adventures. And from the sound of it, they're not too far from the truth."

He imagined her amused smile.

To the left, a pond appeared, a small waterfall feeding it. But he hardly saw either. His sister was one of the smartest people he knew. What she wasn't writing stood out like a lantern at midnight.

Back home, their city must be in a terrible mess for her to not once mention the doings in it. Several notable men lay dead. The only witness to what happened was missing. And those hunting her hadn't found a clue.

His sister would surely have told him if they had.

He chuckled as Bessie's little feet padded along beside him. It was very much like the situation they now faced.

Should he have involved his wife with this murder in a speakeasy? Or had George been right? Was this too dangerous for them?

He shrugged to himself, knowing no one might see. They were in it, and once his wife got her mind set on something, wild horses couldn't drag her away.

They crossed a small bridge over a narrow, gently rushing creek, the windows of the hallway beside this place peeking through the shrubbery. Far ahead, Duchess Cordelia Stayman sat on a bench where the path turned back towards the door.

She was normally optimistic, lively, upbeat. But today, she sat quietly, face downcast, even the beaded strands on her day gown drooping.

Perhaps feeling the somber mood, Bessie stopped, gazing up at him, and he took the little dog into his arms, kissing her curly black hair.

Duchess Cordelia looked over, voice full of emotion. "My dear Mr. Jackson. Come, you won't be a bother."

Mr. Jackson put Bessie down and walked over to her. "I hope you're well?"

She sighed. "Not really. Sit beside me, if you will."

He sat, Bessie beside his feet, her head upon his black leather shoe. "What troubles you, my Lady?"

Duchess Cordelia shrugged. "Today would be our fourth anniversary."

And now her Albert, his friend, would never return. A tinge of melancholy struck. "I'm sorry."

"Sitting here, in the place he loved ... well, it makes me feel closer to him somehow."

Mr. Jackson nodded.

She placed a lined hand on his. "Enough of this. How is my favorite little family?"

He chuckled at that. Bessie had become like a child to them. "Everyone is quite well."

She patted his hand. "Good." She set her hands in her lap. "I suppose they have you wrapped up in this thing downstairs."

He laughed. "Nothing escapes you, does it?"

"Well, this is my place just as much as it is Monty's," she said firmly. "I live here, and it's my duty to keep up with the goings-on."

"You are a delight!"

The old woman blushed. "Why, thank you, sir."

"If you don't mind me asking: what have you learned?" With any luck, she'd know something useful. "It could be ever so helpful."

"Not much," she admitted. "But when I went out for my morning constitutional — and today, it was quite cold! — the new Head Valet, Harry — you know Harry, right? The redhead?"

"Of course," Mr. Jackson said.

"Yes. Well, Harry was talking to the other valet. Charlie, I think it is. In any case, I happened to hear Harry say that his neighbor was there! In that bar! Last night! And he saw a cute little platinum blonde **slap** the man who died!" She stopped, evidently considering this. Then she looked up at him. "Do you think she could have done it? Killed the man?"

Mr. Jackson chuckled. "A woman? Why would you think **that**?"

"Well, it's all over the place. One of the patrolmen that was here last night is married to the maid for tenth floor's second cousin, and the maid of course called to find out what'd happened as soon as she heard."

He laughed. "I see."

"And of course she told all the other maids at luncheon that a woman did it, and Lela told me when she was dressing me just now."

"That makes sense. Did Harry's neighbor happen to know this woman's name?"

"Well, I don't know!" She blushed, embarrassed. "I was listening when I shouldn't have. Should I ask?"

"Not at all," Mr. Jackson said. "It'd be best if I asked him myself."

"Perfectly right," Duchess Cordelia said. "It'd be much more proper if you were to, rather than me."

"I'm glad you think so." Mr. Jackson wondered how he might bring the matter up with their new Head Valet.

Bessie yawned, and Mr. Jackson wondered how much sleep a new mother of puppies might get, even these many days out. His sister hadn't gotten much sleep with hers, and she'd had them one at a time. He rose, offering his hand. "Care to accompany us back to the lobby?"

She rose, with her mood seemingly improved. "I daresay I will!"

When he returned Bessie to their rooms, his wife was bundled up on the parlor sofa in a thick robe, with a freshly lit fire going. "My word, it's gotten cold out! Even colder than this morning!"

He freed Bessie to return to her puppies. "At the suggestion of the veterinarian, we took our walk in the gardens. And guess who we saw there?"

"Cordelia," his wife said warmly. "How is she?"

He sat beside her, going over the entire conversation in his mind. "Ah. Missing dear Albert, of course."

"Pity that."

"But ... she did have news about our little to-do downstairs."

"Really."

"Apparently it's all over the Hotel staff that a woman did it, and a 'cute little platinum blonde' was seen slapping our poor fellow before he died."

She coughed, raspy and deep. "That's interesting."

"Guess the man wasn't too popular with the ladies."

She laughed, and it turned into a coughing fit. Which concerned him. "Sounds more like he was a little **too** popular with the ladies."

"A woman scorned, perhaps?"

"Yet one who from the description couldn't have killed him."

"Because of her height?"

"Well, yes. But with that hair, she would've definitely made an impression on our bartender, particularly if she were sitting beside a man who's now dead."

"True." He hadn't noticed, really, before now. But dark hair was surely more in fashion these days for women. The colorists had signs out everywhere. "Are you well?"

She shrugged. "It's just a cough, that's all. Smoking seems to help."

"Well, I don't like it." He got up, went to the phone. When he returned, she hadn't moved, still gazing at the fire. "The doctor will be along shortly."

She laughed. "Shame on you! That poor man. To force him to go out on a holiday. And in this weather?" She fished in her robe pocket, handed over a folded paper. "This came for you while you were out."

He opened a full piece of notepad paper with a long list of names on it.

"Of course, they all deny to the police they were in a speakeasy last night. But they visited the hospital for various things related to being shoved down in a stampede: a broken nose, a twisted ankle. Or else, they were mentioned as being seen in the club by one of the staff. Regulars, if you will." His wife drew her robe more tightly around her. "He's marked those with a star."

Regulars might know who this dead fellow was. He folded the paper, put it in his pocket. "Excellent."

***

The doctor, who was on retainer with the Hotel, came shortly after. "Bronchitis," he said. "I've seen a dozen of these this week, what with the weather." He left a medicine for the cough. "If she runs a fever, get some Aspirin from the pharmacy. But do call if she's not well in a week."

So he phoned Mr. Vienna and Mrs. Knight, telling them that his wife was ill; they were staying in for dinner and most likely breakfast as well. Then he called to make sure they were paid anyway.

Later that evening, he telephoned Club Patruni to ask for Miss Denton. "My wife is sick, and tomorrow I must go out. Would you stop by to check on her?"

"Is it serious?"

"The doctor doesn't think so."

"Okay." Band music roared in the background. "I gotta go."

"Thanks for your help."

The line clicked. He laughed.

The next morning, he let his wife sleep late, and although she was a bit put out at missing her appointment with the young Head Chef, she did seem better. So after telling her not to expect him until after dinner, Mr. Jackson went to the manager.

Mr. Flannery Davis appeared to be hard at work, far too much so to get up when Mr. Jackson entered. But he did offer a chair. "Please, sit down." He put down his pen. "What can I do for you?"

"I'd like a reckoning of our bill, if you please. I recall you offered us a week's stay when we first arrived, but it's gone well past that."

Mr. Davis blinked. "Is there a problem?"

"Not at all, but I prefer to keep up with my accounts. We've been at the Myriad twice, this last time for several months. I presume at some point, you'd like to be paid?"

The man seemed at a loss for words. "Well ... yes! But Mr. Carlo said —"

"Mr. Carlo is not my concern." Although it was a slight lie, it wouldn't do to show his hand just yet. "I'd like to pay my bill. See to it at once. And I'd like a bill once a month from here on out." Now what would be the best way to do this? "Would you give me your bank information, so I might have the sum transferred?"

"Uh ..." Mr. Davis stared at him blankly, mouth open. "I suppose." He fished around in his desk, then copied some numbers onto a paper. "This is the routing number, and this is the number for the account."

"Very good. Please have the bill sent to my room."

To Mr. Jackson's surprise, Mr. Davis stood, holding out his hand. "Very good, sir! I'll speak to Mr. Carlo about it at once."

Out in the hallway, Mr. Jackson chuckled, shaking his head. He wondered what Mr. Carlo was going to think of all this.

13

M r. Jackson went to the front desk, where a young man with brown hair stood ready. "Do you have a pay phone handy?"

"There's one over there," the clerk said. He pointed to a small door embedded into the wall, between the gift shop and the front of the building.

He gaped at it. "How have I never seen that before?"

"Heh," the clerk said. His tag read: Leo. "Probably because you never needed it 'til now."

"True. By the way, do you have change for a dollar?"

***

As Mr. Jackson had said he'd be gone the day, Mrs. Jackson decided to have a relaxing day of her own.

She soaked in the tub (without wetting her hair, so she didn't have to use that awful heavy dryer). She ordered breakfast in her rooms.

She took Bessie for a walk in the gardens. A young man she didn't recognize strolled far on the other path towards the exit with his child, a brown-haired boy of four or so, skipping beside him.

And she was reminded of her son.

Bessie stopped, peering at her.

She picked the little dog up, holding her there in the middle of the walkway as the tears flowed. *My baby!*

How could she bear to never see him again?

The tears turned to deep, raspy coughing. Bessie began to squirm, so Mrs. Jackson put her down, walking to the little bridge over the even smaller creek. A railing made of stout branches stood there, and she held onto it for a while, watching the rushing water.

She had to accept it. She could never see him again.

If only he could have grown up like that little boy, living happily with his father! No matter what her Mr. Jackson said, she couldn't help thinking her husband's death had been her fault.

She walked along past small trees, flowers, shrubbery, and gradually, she felt calmer. The garden wasn't nearly so well cared-for now that Albert Stayman was gone.

Another loss.

She sat at Duchess Cordelia's favorite bench, near where the tree her husband Albert planted used to be, now also gone.

The ancients said time healed you. But she wished time would get busy. She felt tired of crying all the time.

I'll visit Cordelia, she thought. Maybe that'll help.

She found the dowager in her favorite place, the library, reading a novel. The old woman beamed when she saw her. "Oh, my dear Mrs. Jackson!"

Everyone else in the room turned to frown at them.

"Oh," Cordelia said in a whisper, "I always forget."

Mrs. Jackson smiled warmly at her. "Let's go outside." She and Bessie led Cordelia out to the lobby. "Care for a soda?"

"I suppose."

This was not like Cordelia at all! Taking the old woman's arm, she brought her to the soda shop. "Have you been here before?"

"With my Albert once. He's not fond of sweets, so we never came back."

"But did **you** like it?"

"I suppose I did." She gave a slight smile, then sighed. "Let's see what they have."

Hundreds of bottles holding various colors of liquid sat in a vast array along the walls, clear to the ceiling. In the corner high at the right-hand ceiling behind the counter, a large stuffed owl held residence over the door.

Apparently the owl would blink when a shipment came for the speakeasy. At least, that's what her Mr. Jackson had told her.

The young man behind the counter said, "What can I get for you ladies?"

Mrs. Jackson turned to Cordelia.

"Oh!" Cordelia looked surprised. "I don't know."

"A root beer float for me," said Mrs. Jackson.

"I've never had that," Cordelia said. "Make that two."

"Put the charge to my room," Mrs. Jackson said, "3205. And take a tip for yourself, if you please."

The young man beamed. "Right away!"

They went to one of the small tables and sat. Two couples also sat in the room, but one left a moment after. Cordelia sighed. "They remind me so much of Albert and I." But then she smiled. "Thank you for reminding me there is life without him."

Every little thing must make her recall their time together, Mrs. Jackson thought. Particularly still living here, where they'd been happy. She took the older woman's hand. "It all happened so suddenly. The whole thing's terribly difficult to take in."

Cordelia nodded, reaching for her handkerchief to brush at her cheek.

The young man came up with two tall glasses, each with a straw and a spoon. Setting them down, he brought out the receipt for her to sign, then returned to his post.

Mrs. Jackson and Cordelia sipped their drinks in silence, Bessie nestled beside them. The dowager's situation was such an echo of hers. Yet the poor woman had only empty rooms for company. "My Lady, do you like animals?"

Cordelia smiled warmly at Bessie. "I do, very much!"

"Once we're finished, I have something to show you."

14

The three returned to Mrs. Jackson's parlor. Upon being freed from the leash, little Bessie rushed into Mr. Jackson's bathroom. The two women followed.

Cordelia gasped in delight when she saw what lay there. "Puppies!" She turned to Mrs. Jackson, hands to her mouth. "Why did you never tell me?"

Mrs. Jackson felt amused. "We weren't sure what Mr. Carlo might think. Besides, it's perfectly natural, don't you agree?"

But the dowager Duchess Cordelia Stayman was on her knees in her heavily beaded day dress cooing at the little creatures. "Oh, my stars, they're adorable!"

Mrs. Jackson chuckled. "The spotted one's already spoken for. But you may have whichever of the rest you wish. As soon as they're old enough, of course!"

Cordelia sat upon the tile floor, leaning upon one hand. "That golden one reminds me so much of Albert's hair when we were young." She sighed, but it was wistful now, not sad. "I'll name him Bertie." Tears came to her eyes. "To remember my Albert by."

Mrs. Jackson squatted beside her and took her other hand. "I think that's admirable."

The golden pup wobbled, staring up at them with unfocused eyes. Bessie lay upon her side, eyes closed, as her children made their way to her.

"Well," Mrs. Jackson said, "It'll be a few months before he's ready to leave his mother. But you may visit every day if you wish."

Cordelia sat up, clasping her hands under her chin. "I would so enjoy that."

Mrs. Jackson helped the dowager to her feet.

"They look so well-cared for," Cordelia said. "And so well-fed, too."

Mrs. Jackson smiled fondly at the little family. "They have a good mother."

A knock on the parlor door surprised her. "Please, have a seat in the parlor," said Mrs. Jackson. "I'll see who this is."

She was surprised to see Miss Ophelia Denton at the door. "Oh, my dear Pet!" She gave the young woman a hug, then drew back. "Please, come in!"

The two walked into the parlor; the dowager still stood in the middle of the room.

Mrs. Jackson said, "I'm sure you remember Duchess Cordelia Stayman —"

Ophelia curtsied. "Of course!"

This made Duchess Cordelia laugh. "Now, now, none of that bother." She reached out her hand. "It's so good to see you again."

Mrs. Jackson said, "Come, both of you, sit down." Once they'd sat, she said, "What brings you here?"

"Mr. Hector said you were sick, and I should come check on you." She glanced at the dowager, then back. "But you look okay to me."

As if on cue, a rasping cough burst from deep within. "I feel fine."

"Goodness!" Cordelia looked appalled. "That cough sounds terrible."

This made Mrs. Jackson laugh, which turned once more into coughing. "I feel perfectly well, I swear to you! The doctor said bronchitis, and he left a medicine."

Ophelia's pretty face turned severe. "And are you **taking** it?"

"Silly girl," Mrs. Jackson said. "Of course I am!" She patted the younger woman's hand. "The cough is quite improved, really."

Tears came to Ophelia's eyes; she threw herself into Mrs. Jackson's arms. "My whole family died of a cough just like that," Ophelia sobbed. "I won't lose you too."

Mrs. Jackson patted Ophelia on the back, looking to Duchess Cordelia.

"I'm afraid I'll have to side with Miss Ophelia on this one," the dowager said. "You should **not** be out roaming about if you're ill, not even in the Hotel. You're still young! And you have your husband and friends to think about, not to mention those dear little dogs." She rose. "I'll order you some tea. Lemon and honey are good for the lungs —"

"Not too much honey," Mrs. Jackson said, "I can't abide the taste of it in tea."

"Well, you can have some on a spoon then. But we must get you well!"

After a flurry of activity — including another hot bath — Mrs. Jackson found herself bundled into her robe and slippers (both courtesy of the Hotel) and seated in front of the parlor fireplace.

Wisely, Bessie stayed out of the commotion, only emerging from time to time to ensure all was well.

Ophelia turned off the hair dryer and fluffed Mrs. Jackson's hair. Duchess Cordelia handed her a cup of lemon tea and a spoon (full of honey). "Now," Duchess Cordelia said, "we shall restore you to health."

***

The pay phone cubicle was barely large enough to sit in. Consulting the telephone book, Mr. Jackson had been contacting the people on the list.

But he wasn't having much more luck than Sergeant Nestor did.

"Why would I tell you anything?"

"Are you with the police? I don't have nothing to do with police."

"Oh, no, mister — I'm staying well out of this one."

But then this last man said something strange. "You should become an announcer! You've got a great voice for it."

This he found quite amusing.

Finally, after meeting with the few who would meet with him, and eating at a little diner along the way, he returned to the speakeasy, well after dark. He found one of the bandsmen setting up for the night's show.

"Sure, I saw the little blonde slap him. Don't blame her, the way he carried on! Been here three nights running, with a different gal on his arm every night."

Interesting, Mr. Jackson thought. The bartender acted like he'd never seen the dead man before. "You know the man's name?"

He pulled a chair into place. "Nope."

"What did the other women look like?"

"All the same, really — light skin, brown hair. On the tall side."

"Would you know the last one if you saw her again?"

"Mister, you ever been up on stage? These lights make it hard to see anybody out there clear like."

Mr. Jackson sighed internally. "Would you happen to know the blonde's name?"

"No, but my girl might."

His "girl" was one of the waitresses, a saucy overpainted woman half the bandsman's age. "Why would I give a man information about her?"

"To be honest," Mr. Jackson said wearily, "I don't care much about her."

The young woman's eyebrows raised, looking quite the skeptic.

"I'm just trying to figure out who this dead guy is."

She seemed surprised at that, and after a moment's thought, said, "I won't have some man going round asking for her. She's a good girl: I won't be the one to give her a reputation."

"Not even to get word to her that her man's dead?"

The woman put her hands on her hips. "You really want her to find out that way?"

At that, he felt foolish. "You're absolutely right. Forgive me." What was he to do now? "May my wife call on you, then? Somewhere not here."

She shrugged. "Sure." But she didn't move to write anything down. "Why can't she just come down here?"

He hesitated. "She ... well, she came to grief over alcohol several years back, and —"

The young woman gave a sharp nod. "Gotcha." She went over to the bar and wrote a number on a paper napkin. "Who's gonna be calling? So I know it's her."

For an instant, he forgot what his wife's name here was. Then it came to him. "Pamela Jackson."

She handed over the napkin. On it said, "Calliope," and a number.

He took Calliope's hand. "Thank you. Very much."

She looked into his eyes. "You seem like a good guy. Don't make me out to be wrong."

He smiled at her. "You have my word, miss, I'll not make a move to contact either of you."

She turned away. "Have your missus call before six. But not before noon." She grinned at him over her shoulder. "That is, if she wants me to answer."

***

Duchess Cordelia and Ophelia Denton refused to leave until Mr. Jackson returned. So they had luncheon, tea, and dinner together, interspersed with calls downstairs for one thing or another.

When her Mr. Jackson finally appeared, Mrs. Jackson was stretched out on the sofa with a poultice on her chest and a hot rag on her forehead, feeling quite fussed over.

Mr. Jackson, on the other hand, looked more than a little surprised. "Whatever is going on here?"

Duchess Cordelia frowned at him. Frowned! "You should be ashamed of yourself, sir, for leaving your wife in such a state. She was out and about! Sick as she was!"

Ophelia nodded.

Mrs. Jackson laughed. "They've made me a project! I happened to cough, and got pounced upon."

Ophelia said, "You were in the worst coughing fit I've heard in some time!" Angry tears came to her eyes once more. "It's no laughing matter!"

Mrs. Jackson felt chagrined. "Come, Pet."

The young woman came and knelt before her.

Mrs. Jackson took her into her arms, laying her head upon her shoulder. "I'm sorry to make light of this, I really am. Look at me." Taking the girl's tear-streaked face in her hands, she said, "I don't plan to die any time soon. The doctor's been here, and he said if I got worse, to call. Many people this week have this thing I have, and it's because of the weather, not flu." She peered into Ophelia's eyes. "You hear me? I'm still right here."

Ophelia smiled at that. "I'm sorry to fret so."

"You fret because you care about her," said Duchess Cordelia. "As do I."

Mr. Jackson stood there, mouth open. Finally, he said, "Forgive me; I never meant to burden you ladies with this." He came over to stand beside her. "I'll not leave until she's well."

That set them both to mumblings:

"Oh, it's been no burden —"

"It's no bother, really —"

"Thank you," Mrs. Jackson said, clasping Ophelia's hand with one hand and Duchess Cordelia's with the other. "I feel much better." And she did. Maybe this tending-to was what she needed. "It really has been lovely to spend the day together." A wave of tiredness came over her. "But I think I'll be off to bed now."

Once they left, she discarded the poultice and the rag (both of which had gone cold), and let her Mr. Jackson put her to bed. There he sat, telling her the story of his day. "Let me see if Sergeant Nestor might come by, this time without breaking into our bedrooms."

That made her laugh.

***

When Mr. Jackson called that night to let Mrs. Knight know his wife was still sick, the woman offered to come care for his wife the next day. "I've been a nursemaid before," she said, "and my other appointment for today has cancelled."

So he called Monsieur to apprise him of the situation.

The sound of pots and pans lay far in the background. "When I heard her cough, I knew it was serious."

"The doctor said it was just bronchitis."

"Many died of the flu when I was in Paris," Monsieur said. "I wouldn't take any such cough lightly."

And Mr. Carlo's daughter was ill as well.

Mr. Jackson began to feel concerned. "I have a nursemaid coming in the morning," he said, "if she's not improved I may call the doctor back."

"Good idea," Monsieur said. "Let me know how I might help."

"I will." He never considered that coming here might expose his wife to contagion! Of all the things to have to worry about, he thought. Going to his wife's room, he found her sleeping, so he lay down beside her.

She had no fever, nor did she act unwell. He wrapped his arm around her, laying his head close to hers. He didn't know if he could bear to lose her, now that they were finally happy.

15

When Mrs. Jackson woke, Mr. Jackson sat dressed for the street, drinking coffee and reading the news. "Good morning," he said cheerfully.

The sound of water running in the sink came from her bathroom. "What's going on?"

"Mrs. Knight has informed me that she's an experienced nursemaid. So I've asked her to give us an opinion on the matter and care for you today."

"I don't feel sick," she said, then began coughing. It did rather rattle in her chest a bit.

Mrs. Knight came in from the bathroom. "I don't like the sound of that at all."

"Smoking helps the most. And that medicine of the doctor's helps calm it as well."

Mrs. Knight glanced at Mr. Jackson. "Any fever?"

"No," Mrs. Jackson said, before he might reply. "Nor any other symptom."

"My pardons, ma'am," said Mrs. Knight. "But sometimes you can have a fever when you're asleep, and never know it."

Mrs. Jackson felt reproved.

"Not that I've seen," Mr. Jackson said, and he sounded concerned. "Is that important?"

Mrs. Knight let out a breath. "Flu is unlikely without fever, usually one that's quite high."

Mr. Jackson said, "That's a relief."

"Have you coughed blood?"

Mrs. Jackson stared at Mrs. Knight, suddenly frightened. "No, never!"

"Then the doctor is likely correct: you have bronchitis." Mrs. Knight smiled warmly. "A few days' rest and you should be good as new."

"All this fuss over nothing," Mrs. Jackson grumbled.

"You still must rest," said Mrs. Knight. "You won't recover otherwise." She went to the bathroom.

A laugh burst from Mr. Jackson.

"What is it?"

"Just remembering how hard it was to get you to rest when you had your surgery," he said.

Must he bring that up now? "I promise to, if only for Ophelia's sake. The poor dear — I regret worrying her."

Mrs. Knight returned with a towel; two poultices lay upon it.

"Duchess Cordelia put one of those on me," Mrs. Jackson said.

"Did she now?"

"Just last night."

"Huh," Mrs. Knight said, sounding impressed. "I'd like to hear the story of where a Duchess learned nursecraft." She lifted one of the cloths. "Come now, let's put this one on your back."

***

Mr. Jackson called the sergeant to let him know of the delay. It took twenty minutes to get the man on the line.

And when he did, it sounded like an entire crowd was in the background.

"It's just as well," Sergeant Nestor said. "We're terribly busy. Because of the holiday, you see." He scoffed. "The autopsy-man has a whole list of them to do. He took the man's fingerprints, but won't get to a proper study until tomorrow at the earliest. Never mind us — you take care of your wife."

The man hung up before Mr. Jackson could tell him about the blonde. It didn't seem really enough to go through all that waiting again, so he returned to sit beside his wife. She was sitting up in bed in her nightgown, legs straight out, bent over so her face nearly touched her knees, having her back pounded upon.

"Brings up the phlegm," Mrs. Knight said as she pounded. "That's the trouble with these medicines the doctors give. They calm the cough. But the cough's purpose is to bring out the infection inside, so it doesn't fester into pneumonia."

"Oh." Mr. Jackson felt chagrined. "So ... did he advise us wrongly?"

"Not at all," said Mrs. Knight. "The medicine is wonderful for helping the patient sleep. But more is sometimes needed in cases like hers."

His wife coughed, and it did sound better. "I'm grateful you're here for her."

Mrs. Knight looked quite pleased. "Thank you, sir." To his wife, she said, "Now let's roll onto your left side."

"I feel like a side of beef," his wife said. She grinned. "I shall be quite tenderized."

Mr. Jackson laughed, kneeling beside her. He kissed her forehead. "You really are a silly old girl." He smoothed her hair, feeling a great fondness for her.

"What did the sergeant say?"

"He sounded up to his ears in work!"

"Ah," his wife said. "The holiday."

"Right you are. So nothing will be done, or come back, or whatever, until tomorrow at the earliest."

She chuckled. "This place is ever so modern. But it seems some things never change."

***

Once the pounding finished, Mrs. Jackson did feel better. The couple called up for luncheon, ordering some for Mrs. Knight as well.

It being after noon, Mrs. Jackson gave this Miss Calliope a call. The woman agreed to meet at a local bistro two days hence for a late luncheon, on the condition that Mrs. Jackson pay.

That seemed most amusing.

With the pounding and poultices and steam heat, and Mr. Jackson hardly leaving her side, soon Mrs. Jackson was her old self again. Everyone agreed she was fit to go out, she thought none too soon.

On the way to meet with Miss Calliope, she went to a chapel, lighting a candle for Mr. Carlo's daughter Margaret's healing as well.

16

Calliope Washington was past the large salad — with everything on it — and into an equally large sandwich. "Didn't think you were real."

And she'd ordered dessert!

Mrs. Jackson sampled her chowder, wondering how the woman kept her figure. "I most certainly am. What can you tell me about the man who died?"

Calliope grinned at her around a mouthful of food, then swallowed, wiping her lips. "Straight to the point, are we?"

Mrs. Jackson dropped an oyster cracker to Bessie, who snapped it up. "I tend to be." She chuckled to herself. "You know his young lady well, I take it."

Calliope shrugged. "She used to waitress at the Myriad. In the restaurant, until the old guy took a fancy to her and told her she'd get better tips downstairs." She took a long drink of her soda. "She didn't want to at first — her ma's a teetotaler — but I told her what her ma don't know won't hurt her."

Mrs. Jackson laughed. "Her ma never comes to visit?"

"Oh, no — they don't have that kind of money. It's hard to even get a reservation for breakfast these days."

"I see."

"So anyway, about a year later, she took a job at this other place that paid better. I guess that's where she met the guy."

"Any idea what his name is?"

"Aaron something." She shook her head, frowning. "Can't remember. She can tell you all that."

"So you didn't socialize?"

She pushed the sandwich plate aside and gestured for dessert. "Sure, we went out on the town, the days we all weren't working."

The waiter brought a huge slice of chocolate cake and set it before her.

"Coffee, if you please," Calliope said.

The waiter turned to Mrs. Jackson. "And anything else for you, ma'am?"

She'd finished her soup. "Tea would be lovely." She turned to Calliope. "Did you see what happened?"

She shook her head. "I didn't even see him, or the gal he was with, that's how busy we were." She took a bite of cake, swallowed. "I've been there three years and never seen the place so full."

"That's what they tell me."

Calliope had already eaten a third of the cake. Once the waiter had gone, she gestured with her fork. "We don't tend to give out names like you lot do. And you're never sure if someone's giving you the right name anyway. He said call him Aaron, so that's what we called him." She shook her head. "They're saying that that last gal was the one who shot him."

Mrs. Jackson didn't think it would hurt to admit it, so she nodded.

"Hell of a way to go, even if he did break her heart."

Mrs. Jackson understood that feeling all too well. She leaned forward. "I don't mean your friend any harm. The police don't even have to know her name if she doesn't want it. But I don't feel right not finding out anything that might help them learn who did this."

Calliope set down her fork, eyes on her plate. After a moment, she nodded. "Her name's Trixie. Quinlan. And she lives right down the street, by the El train."

***

Trixie Quinlan was maybe twenty and at three in the afternoon, still in her bathrobe. She beamed when she saw Bessie. She cried when told the news. "I wish I'd never left him that way," she sobbed. "I told him he was rotten, good for nothing. That was the last he heard me say. I'd take it back if I could."

They were sitting at a wobbly wooden table in the center of a dismal little one-room: a bed up against a wall and a pot-bellied stove in the corner. The window beside the dresser looked out onto a window from the other building and the brick around it. Mrs. Jackson took her hand. "I'm sorry."

Trixie nodded, her eyes upon the large doily covering most of the table. Something an older woman might make, if given the time. "I loved him. I truly loved him. Why did he **do** that?"

"Men do strange things sometimes."

Trixie bit her lip, eyes wide, staring. Then tears filled them again, began to drop upon her lap.

"What happened?"

"What do you mean?"

"On New Year's Eve. I heard you slapped him."

"I did. One of the other waitresses where I work said she'd just done a shift at the Myriad and saw him there with another girl. So I left. I went there and used her code to get in. There he was!" She started to cry again. "He never even said he was sorry."

"What was she like?"

"Thin, brown hair. And she was old! At least thirty. Not even pretty, either."

The poor girl must feel humiliated. "Would you know her if you saw her again?"

"Oh, yes," Trixie said. "I've seen her hanging round work before this. But I better not see her again, or I'll give her a piece of my mind!"

Mrs. Jackson said, "Is there someone who can come stay with you? Or a place you can go?"

She was quiet for some time "My mother lives in Pilsen." She nodded, wiped her nose. "Ma'll say I told you so. But I'll go home."

"It'd be good to have someone with you right now."

"Will there be a funeral?"

Mrs. Jackson shrugged. "So far they don't even know his name. I came here to find out who he was."

Trixie gasped, hands to her mouth. "All this time, and they didn't even know his **name**? It's Aaron Lucas! I'm pretty sure he lives on the East Side."

"You've never been to his house?"

"What kind of girl do you **take** me for? Of course not! And before you ask, he's never been in here, either." She gave a satisfied nod.

Interesting. "How long were you together?"

"Almost a year," she said. "We met at the Mulder. That's where I work."

Mrs. Jackson nodded. Sergeant Nestor would know where that was. "I have to ask. Or else the police will want to. Where were you on New Year's Eve?"

"When I got home my landlady gave me a message."

"What message?"

"I got fired for leaving like I did." Trixie's face grew somber. "Never been fired from anything before." She stared towards the table. "I bought a bottle. I was here. Drinking. Until daybreak. I never felt so low in my life."

"Did anyone see you?"

She let out a laugh, gesturing to the window across the way. "Half the city was in that party over there. Every so often a different one of them would lean out and tell me to come over. But I never did."

All easily verifiable. She didn't think this girl could have killed the man anyway. "So what did your Mr. Lucas do? For a living?"

"Oh, he was an accountant."

"Really? Where did he work?"

Trixie's face became evasive. "On his own. He had his own business, out of his home, doing books for people. He was really busy." She pointed to a framed, half page magazine clipping with a photo of the man and a headline: Aaron Lucas: Rising Star. "He said business was good! Really good. He always showed me a real good time."

Mrs. Jackson smiled to herself. "That sounds lovely. Can you give me your mother's number in case we need to get hold of you? Like if the police need you to identify the body."

Her hands went to her mouth. "Oh. Does he look really awful?"

"I haven't seen him, but he's surely been cleaned up by this time. No blood or anything like that." She tried to make her voice reassuring. "It's only if they can't find any next of kin. To make sure it's really your Aaron, and not someone else that only looks like him."

She nodded. "I see." She rose, went to the dresser, wrote on a piece of paper, handed it over. "Yes, please call me. I want to be at his funeral."

17

Mrs. Jackson went back to the Hotel. She'd have an easier time with what came next if Mr. Jackson accompanied her.

After returning Bessie to her puppies, she found Mr. Jackson in his room reading the afternoon paper. He glanced up. "There you are! Have any luck?"

"I have. Let's call to see if the sergeant is in."

Luckily for them, Sergeant Nestor was indeed in. When they arrived at the station, the couple were shown back at once.

The place was utilitarian, yet busy. Sergeant Nestor's office was no different.

The sergeant was occupied with papers when they were shown in. "There you are! Good to see you looking well. Have a seat." He finished writing, then set down his pen. "What have you learned?"

Mrs. Jackson opened her mouth to speak.

Mr. Jackson said, "One of the men in the band saw a short blonde woman slap the dead fellow a few days before he died."

"And?"

Mrs. Jackson, amused, waited for Mr. Jackson to turn to her expectantly. Then waited just a bit more. "Our young lady's name," she said calmly, "is Trixie Quinlan.

She says the dead man is an independent accountant named Aaron Lucas. She even has a magazine clipping using that name with the man's portrait. They've been together almost a year, and she's never been to his home. She thinks he lives on the East Side. At least a dozen people saw her at home on New Year's Eve, well until dawn." At that, she felt sad. "She's on her way to her mother's house in Pilsen," she fished out the slip of paper, "and she's willing to come identify the body if there's no next of kin."

The sergeant took the slip of paper. "Interesting."

Mr. Jackson leaned forward. "How so?"

"Because the dead man's fingerprints came back. His name is actually Mark Boyle, and he's done time for embezzling."

***

Mr. Jackson felt astonished. "**He's** done time, too?"

The sergeant nodded, pulling out a file from his drawer and opening it; the dead man's portrait lay inside. "Same place as our bartender, but in different lockups. It's doubtful that they ever met. No, embezzling carries a much higher charge: Mr. Boyle here got fifteen years, out in ten for good behavior." He squinted at the page. "Says here he got out a little over a year ago."

Mrs. Jackson said, "Right before he met Trixie."

Mr. Jackson said, "The bandsman saw Mr. Boyle there three nights running, with a different girl on his arm each night."

Sergeant Nestor let out a laugh. "That explains all the lipstick." He leaned forward. "Where'd she know him?"

"I knew I forgot something," his wife said. "At the Mulder. She works there. That's where they met."

The sergeant nodded. "I know the place."

"The girl she found him with goes there as well," his wife said. "A thin unattractive woman at least my age with brown hair."

"Shouldn't be too hard to find her at the Mulder, if she's there a lot," Sergeant Nestor said. "Did she give you a name for this woman?"

His wife shook her head.

"Well," the sergeant said, "I better go have a talk with the Mulder, and see if they can tell me more about this woman. Or our 'Mr. Lucas' here."

"I'm curious," Mr. Jackson said. "What else did you find? About the card? The phone number?"

"No one's answering the phone number," Sergeant Nestor said. "I'm having the phone company track down the address. The repair shop recognized Mr. Boyle; he'd come in asking about getting his lighter fixed."

Ah, he thought. "So he might have left it there?"

"Nope," the sergeant said. "He said he'd think about it and took the card."

His wife let out a laugh.

But Mr. Jackson felt curious about another matter. "Did his autopsy show anything?"

The sergeant shrugged. "As we thought, he'd been drugged. Your usual sleeping powder — you can find it at any pharmacy. But it needs a prescription, so that'll help narrow down any suspects we find."

That sounded helpful. Mr. Jackson said, "Anything else you'd like us to do?"

"Not a present," said the sergeant.

"Oh," his wife said. "Miss Quinlan would like to be notified about the funeral."

"We gotta find the man's next of kin first," the sergeant said. "We're having trouble tracking anyone down. But I'll let you know."

So with that, the couple went back to the Hotel.

"It's odd," Mr. Jackson said, once they were back in their parlor. "Your Miss Trixie was with the man almost a year and didn't know his real name."

He regretted saying so almost immediately. From the look on his wife's face, this case was coming much too close to home for her liking.

Feeling a surge of compassion, he took her in his arms. "Forgive me; I'd forgotten all that happened." Yet he didn't know what really went on that night they fled the city.

He felt rather than saw her nod. "She's escaped with her life, her health, and a mother she's willing and able to return to. It's more than many who meet up with such a man can hope for."

This surprised him. But she sounded so forlorn that he didn't want to press her further. "Would you like to go down for an ice cream soda?"

She smiled up at him. "I think that would be lovely."

***

Fetching Bessie, the couple went down for their soda.

Mrs. Jackson did indeed feel that this case came much too close to her own story.

But she'd vowed not to let her past ruin her. She had much to think of today.

Like what magazine would run an article praising a convicted felon? Surely a reputable organization would have checked the man's credentials before running the story. So this could only be some tabloid.

Even so, this whole thing seemed strange.

Once they finished their sodas, she said, "Let's bring our Queen Bess up to her young subjects and have a go at the park, shall we?"

"Very well," Mr. Jackson said. "It might be nice to get outdoors. You go ahead; I have some business with the front desk."

So she brought Bessie to her puppies and returned to the front desk where Mr. Jackson was waiting for her. The park was close by, tree-lined paths and cold air and an overcast sky. And after they'd gone round and were on their way back, coming the other way was none other than Trixie Quinlan!

"They said you'd be out here," Trixie said.

"My goodness," Mrs. Jackson said. "However did you find us?"

She looked embarassed. "Figured you had something to do with the place. So I went to the front and told them we were supposed to meet." She shrugged. "They said you'd just left."

Oh, dear, thought Mrs. Jackson. If she could be found so easily by this slip of a girl, others could find her too. "Was there something we might help you with?"

Trixie peered up at Mr. Jackson. "This must be the man Calliope told me about."

Mr. Jackson tipped his hat. "Hector Jackson, at your service."

Trixie took a deep breath. "There's something I didn't tell you. Back at the house."

The couple waited.

"Um," she said. "I think Aaron was mixed up in something bad."

18

Mr. Jackson, his wife, and little Miss Trixie walked along the park paths as the young woman told her story. They'd met at the Mulder, it was true. And they'd go out every weekend, and most nights she had off. But when he'd take her out on the town, he'd spend a lot of money. Too much money.

"At first it was fun," Miss Trixie said. "Then it started to scare me, especially when we started meeting up with these men." She fell silent.

His wife spoke up. "What kind of men?"

"They were really rich," Miss Trixie said. "They'd talk about jobs, and the men with them had guns. I may be dumb, but I'm not stupid. They had to be hit men. You know, gangsters." She stared down at the path. "I loved him. I didn't want to believe it. When I'd say something about it all, he'd never really lie. They were clients. He was doing work for them. Sure they were rich. He was good at his job, and they paid him well for it." She sighed. "But now he's dead."

Mr. Jackson shook his head. She had to know the truth. "His real name's Mark Boyle —"

Miss Trixie stared up at him, startled. "What?"

"— and when you met him, he'd just gotten out of prison." He felt sorry for the girl. "Ten years for embezzling."

She stopped in the path. "So was everything he told me a lie?"

His wife said gently, "I don't suppose we'll ever know."

The girl — she was very young, nineteen or twenty at most — began to cry, and his wife consoled her, taking Miss Trixie into her arms.

Such a sad story, he thought.

His wife handed the girl a handkerchief (courtesy of the Hotel). "Now, now," she said. "This man isn't worth spoiling your makeup over. Wipe your eyes. We need to get our overcoats, but then we'll take you home."

***

Mrs. Jackson thought that the sight of two-week-old puppies snuggled up next to Bessie might make Trixie feel better.

"Oh, they're so little! And that one looks just her!" She looked up at her. "I wish I could have that little black one. But I don't think my Ma would like that."

Mrs. Jackson stood. "They're not old enough in any case." She adjusted her overcoat. "But let's get everything settled first. In a few months, when they're ready to leave their mother, we can talk about it then."

Trixie stood, gazing down at them. "They remind me of my cousins when they was born."

Mrs. Jackson rested her hand on Trixie's back. "Babies are much the same, wherever you go."

"I want a baby someday." Trixie's tears began to flow once more. "I wanted to marry Aaron," she sobbed, "He said we could have a house together, and a family. And now he's dead."

19

In the taxi on the way to her mother's home, Mr. Jackson watched the girl. Miss Trixie sat stunned, as if everything in her life had gone horribly wrong.

Mr. Jackson said, "We found cigarettes in his pocket."

Miss Trixie nodded.

"Did he have a lighter? Or did he use —"

"Oh, yes," Miss Trixie said. "He had one of those old Pist-o-liters. You know, the kind that looks like a gun?"

They both shook their heads. "It wasn't on him," Mr. Jackson said. "Do you recall anything else about it?"

"It wasn't on him? He used it all the time! Let me see — it's cast iron, kind of heavy. It sort of pulled his pocket down. And it had a piece chipped off the corner of the handle. But loved that thing — he never went anywhere without it. He told me one of his friends gave it to him, way back when."

"Did you ever recall anything about his friends? Like their names?"

She shrugged, downcast. "We met with a lot of guys. And their flappers. None of the girls knew him, though, not until we were introduced. That's what surprised me so much, made me so angry there at the end. He had other girls with him, and I never knew!" She stopped then, staring at her knees. "The one I remember most was a big guy. He never sat down with us. And he kept staring at me. Made me glad Aaron was there. It gave me the heebie-jeebies!" She shuddered. "They called that guy Simon once. But mostly Jasper. I don't know which was his real name." She stared at them, mouth open. "Do you think they were all lying?"

"Hard to say." Mr. Jackson thought it likely, though. "Anything else?"

She gave a one-arm shrug. "I mostly just talked with the girls. But there was this one other man that really scared me, even more than the rest. They met up together right before Aaron died. They called him Mr. Russell, and they sent all us girls to get them drinks when they talked."

"Hmm," Mr. Jackson said, recalling something similar when he was a boy.

"Then when we got the drinks," Miss Trixie said, "They wouldn't let us sit with them! We had to take our own table." She sniffled, just a bit. "I don't mind waitressing. But I didn't like sitting like that by ourselves in some bar, with all those men looking at us like we were the buffet. I told him so later."

"Wait," his wife said. "Wasn't this at the Mulder?"

"No, he didn't like drinking there, 'specially right before he died."

"So where was it?"

She glanced at the cabbie, who seemed a bit too particularly interested. "I'll write it for you."

She opened her bag, taking out a notepad and pencil, then passed a slip to his wife.

They weren't in too bad an area. "We'll get out here." He handed over a bill to the man.

After the cab left, Mr. Jackson flagged down another.

Miss Trixie said, "Why'd you do that?"

After they got in, Mr. Jackson said, "I'm not sure it's a good idea to talk about this right now."

They rode to Pilsen in silence.

That first cabbie knows where we were going, he thought. And it worried him.

Mrs. Quinlan was an older version of the girl, but her hair was long, brown, and up in a bun. Mr. Jackson made introductions. "Might I use your telephone?"

"Certainly."

Mr. Jackson called the Myriad. "Is Mr. Carlo in?"

After a few minutes, Mr. Carlo answered the phone. "What's all this about?"

"You know a fellow named Russell? Has a man called Simon Jasper."

Mr. Carlo gasped.

"I'm taking it that you do. There's a girl with information you'd find interesting. But she's not safe here. One moment." He covered the receiver with his hand. "Mrs. Quinlan, is there somewhere you can go?"

"My sister's in Cicero. What's this all about?"

"Your daughter's in trouble," his wife said, "and it'd be best if you two weren't here for a while."

Mr. Jackson spoke into the telephone. "Would you take her and her mother to Cicero?" He gave the address where they were right now. "And keep an eye on them."

"I'll come for them myself." The line went dead.

That was rather rude, he thought. Then he turned to Mrs. Quinlan. "There's a friend of mine named Mr. Carlo. He's going to take you and your daughter to your sister's and leave men to watch over you."

Mrs. Quinlan nodded. "So it's that kind of trouble. I've heard of Carlo and Russell both." She held out her hands, and Miss Trixie went over to hug her. Arm around her daughter, she looked up at him. "Thank you for helping us."

"My pleasure."

The couple waited at Mrs. Quinlan's kitchen table over tea as the two women packed some clothing, every so often stopping to cry and hug each other.

Mr. Jackson whispered to his wife, "It must be wrenching to have to flee your home at a moments' notice like this, not knowing if the place you go to will be entirely safe either."

She nodded. "It was." But then she smiled. "You've been quite the champion, both times."

He laughed softly, not wanting the ladies to hear. "Thank you. But I'd honestly like to keep everyone safe, if possible."

Finally, Mr. Carlo arrived. Mrs. Quinlan seemed more than a bit awed to meet him, yet also a bit afraid. "Let's sit down a moment," he said, "and my men'll take you and your mother's luggage out to the car."

***

So everyone sat around the kitchen table.

Mrs. Jackson watched as Trixie told her story. Something had happened during that telephone conversation between Mr. Jackson and Mr. Carlo, and she was curious to know what.

Mr. Carlo seemed only to care about this Mr. Russell: where they met, who he had with him, what the dead man was doing for him. "And you say he didn't want to go to the Mulder anymore?"

Trixie shook her head. "No, he didn't even want to step inside that last month. Oh," she said, "I got the name of that other woman: Mabel Franklin."

Mr. Carlo flinched. "What other woman?"

Tears came to her eyes. "The one Aaron was with."

Her mother put an arm around her daughter, handing her a handkerchief.

The girl still used his fake name. "Did he ever say **why** he worked for those men?"

Trixie sighed. "I asked him the same thing, that night we saw Mr. Russell. He said they hired him when no one else would."

From the corner of her eye, she saw Mr. Jackson nodding. That's how these mobsters got people. Promise them a job, money, status. Safety. Then they were trapped. "It sounds like your Aaron was loyal to them."

"He was," Trixie said. "He said he'd do just about anything for them."

Hmm. "Do you want to stop by and see Aaron before you go? I'm not sure how much longer they'll be able to keep the body."

Trixie took her mother's hand. "My ma and my auntie and my little cousins have got dragged into this, all because of me." She sighed. "I knew what sort he was.

But I just didn't want to see it. If anything should happen to them —"

Her mother said, "Oh, honey —"

Mrs. Jackson took Trixie's other hand. "You can't blame yourself. You didn't know this would happen."

It was if the girl didn't hear a word. "Now I've lost everything: my job, my place, everything I had there. And my ma's gotta move, and who knows if my aunt and cousins will have to move? And it's all because of me." She shook her head. "I don't want to see Aaron like that anyway. Dead." She turned away. "I'd rather remember him how he was."

20

When Mr. Carlo had learned all he wanted, he led Mr. Jackson and his wife out front.

Several men and three cars stood at the curb. A burly brown-skinned fellow seemed to lead them; Mr. Carlo gestured for the man to come closer.

This man had a stillness to him, both at rest and in motion, which gave Mr. Jackson the feeling that he stood before some giant ship sailing upon calm water. "This is Mr. James Gray," Mr. Carlo said. "He's been watching for news of you."

Mr. Gray tipped his fedora in one smooth motion. "You'll have plenty of warning should someone discover you're in the city."

Mr. Jackson liked the fellow at once. "We're most grateful, sir."

Miss Trixie and her mother had followed behind. His wife put an arm around Miss Trixie's shoulder. "Keep them safe as can be."

"We will." Mr. Gray smiled warmly at the young woman and her mother. "Now, if you'll point out which items you want moved into storage and which sold —"

Mrs. Quinlan paled, but she nodded, and the three returned inside.

"I'll go with them," Mrs. Jackson said. "This must be a terrible ordeal."

So Mr. Jackson and Mr. Carlo stood on the front porch, taking in the view.

It was a pleasant neighborhood, of brick homes and curious little old ladies pretending to trim front gardens.

Mr. Jackson wondered what was going on with the Mulder. Mark Boyle had obviously been doing the accounts for whoever owned it. Why would he suddenly refuse to drink at his own speakeasy?

Mr. Carlo's voice startled him. "What's happened?"

Mr. Jackson smiled to himself. He'd expected this conversation. "Whatever could you possibly mean?"

"Your bill."

Mr. Jackson chuckled. "I should ask the same question. When I went to the front desk today, your manager — who earlier seemed quite eager to help — now says my bill isn't ready. Is there a problem?"

"Well, no ..." Mr. Carlo seemed at a loss for words. "I thought we had an arrangement."

Mr. Jackson wanted very much to laugh, but thought it best not to. "When we arrived, you quite generously offered us a week's stay. It's been many months past that." He folded his arms. "I'd just like to keep current, if that's all right with you."

Mr. Carlo's eyes narrowed. "I've offended you."

"Not at all, sir. We're here, willing to help in any way we can. But ..." Should he say it? "We don't share the same goals." He gestured out into the neighborhood. "My father had the back room deals, the men on the street corners. Some very much like your Mr. Gray in there. Yet my father's life was ever one of looking over his shoulder, in case some underling wanted to seize power." It'd been something much more mundane that had killed his father. But he wondered at times if the strain of the life his father had chosen might have caused it. "I wish you whatever success you desire. But I have no wish to be part of it. My only goal is for my wife to live free — safe, happy, and in peace."

The women came out front and this time, he did laugh. "Besides, we too might need to disappear one day, and I'd not like your Mr. Gray after us."

Mr. Carlo laughed. "Fair enough." He clapped Mr. Jackson a bit too hard on the shoulder. "I'll have the bill to your room before dinner."

"Thank you, sir."

"Well, to be honest, I could use the money." He glanced aside. "Find out who did this. Every day the speakeasy is closed, with police everywhere ... it's beginning to cost me."

Mr. Jackson nodded. "Sorry we didn't tell you about the dogs. It never occurred to me you might object."

Mr. Carlo shrugged. "I don't think Margaret wants one. But Maisy might. She's home alone all day, and —"

Mr. Jackson smiled to himself. "It'll be months before they're old enough to travel. But she can come by any time she likes and pick one out."

Mr. Gray and the women emerged. Mr. Jackson gestured at the man with his chin, and he came over. "How may I help?"

Mr. Jackson described the taxi ride, and the cabbie who seemed rather too interested in their conversation.

Mr. Gray nodded. "I'll have my guys watch the place. If Russell's men show up, we'll take care of it."

His wife stood off to one side, speaking with the women too quietly to hear. They hugged her, and smiled over at him.

Miss Quinlan and her mother went into one car, the rest of the men into the second. Once they were off, Mr. Carlo rode with Mr. and Mrs. Jackson in the third car, back to the Myriad.

Mrs. Jackson said, "Mr. Boyle would do just **about** anything, huh?"

Mr. Jackson nodded. "I thought the same thing."

Mr. Carlo stared at them. "You think Russell had the man killed."

Mr. Jackson took a deep breath. "It's quite the possibility. If our Mr. Boyle had balked at doing something for them there at the Mulder —"

"Or somewhere else," his wife said.

"Yes, exactly." Mr. Jackson brushed a bit of lint off his fedora, which sat upon his knee. "Tell me more about this man Russell."

Mr. Carlo said, "He's a small man, ex-boxer. The sort who shoots first and asks questions later. The man's got something in his eyes that scares me."

Mr. Jackson thought it touching for a man in Mr. Carlo's position to admit that to them.

"Runs small-time loan sharking and bookie operations on the East Side. But his big thing is liquor. He has speakeasies all up and down the waterfront. Gets in trouble with the other gangs once in a while. But they generally leave him alone."

His wife said, "Why?"

Mr. Carlo seemed surprised. "Why?" He leaned back, hand to chin. "Hmm. That's a good question. I think the man's more interested in money than territory. He's never really bothered me." He seemed to have decided something. "I think the big operations don't consider him a threat."

Mrs. Jackson said, "Are you on good enough terms with," she gestured around with her hand, "that lot to find out whether one of **them** did it?"

"I can try," Mr. Carlo said. Then he relaxed, just a bit. "But I know Mabel Franklin. She's a hitter for hire."

21

All Mr. Jackson could do was to stare at he man. "Really."

Mr. Carlo nodded, with a look on his face that suggested he'd had her do some work for him in the past. "If she'd been hanging around the Mulder, I'd expect she had a target there."

Mr. Jackson expected his wife to be surprised, or perhaps even alarmed.

But instead, she said, "If you can set up a meeting, I'd like to talk with her."

"Heh," said Mr. Carlo. "This'll be interesting."

They arrived at the Myriad Hotel, and Harry came round to open Mr. Carlo's door. But Mr. Carlo waved him away. "Just dropping off."

"Yes, sir." Harry opened the door for Mr. Jackson and his wife.

Once they got out of the car, Mr. Jackson remembered the conversation he'd had with Duchess Cordelia. He took his wife's arm. "Let's wait here a bit."

His wife nodded, taking out a cigarette.

"Why do you want to speak with Mabel Franklin?"

His wife snorted softly. "She sounds like a professional. There's no way she'd be seen out in public, in front of over a hundred people, with the man she was hired to hit, on the night she planned to kill him. So if she **was** there —"

"She likely saw the killer."

His wife nodded.

The couple stood looking out past Lake Shore Drive, past the waterfront, out over the icy lake. Cars came and went, the valets and bellhops moving to and fro.

Once the rush passed and Harry returned to his post, Mr. Jackson said to his wife, "Over here."

Harry, the Myriad's new Head Valet, was a young man with red hair, who grinned when the couple approached. "What can I do for you?"

Mr. Jackson said, "The to-do downstairs the other night. I hear your neighbor was there."

Harry chuckled. "I thought Duchess Cordelia was listening in." He crossed his arms. "Well, what do you want to know?"

Mr. Jackson shrugged. "What all did he tell you? About the murder, I mean."

Harry looked completely surprised, his arms dropping to his side. "I think he would have said if he saw **that**. But there were way too many people in there for him to have seen much."

"Well, he saw the young lady slap him," Mrs. Jackson said. "Did he see the man with anyone else?"

Harry shrugged. "You'd have to ask him." He peered at Mr. Jackson. "I doubt he'd talk to you on his own." He gestured with his chin. "Let me see if he'll meet up with the both of us about it."

Mr. Jackson felt quite pleased. "Splendid idea."

***

The couple went to their rooms, and without even taking their shoes off, cast themselves upon Mrs. Jackson's bed. Bessie came jumping up on the bed to lie between them.

"What a day," Mrs. Jackson said. "Do you think they'll be able to protect little Trixie?"

"Carlo? I imagine so."

Recalling the conversation in the first cab, she felt a certain anxiety for the young woman and her family. If this Mr. Russell learned that Trixie had been speaking to Mr. Carlo ...

"There's nothing more we can do for her," Mr. Jackson said. "Sooner or later, we have to trust him."

She sighed, relaxing. "You're entirely right, as usual."

He chuckled. "But I've decided to pay him what we owe in its entirety. That way, if we need to leave —"

How thoughtful! She rolled to face him. "We won't be bogged down by detail."

He laughed. "Or worse, have Carlo's men after us for the bill." He gazed up towards the ceiling. "But it's been quite the adventure getting this all together. I'll have the money transferred tomorrow."

The room was quite warm. She slid her hand under her pillow, savoring its coolness. "But we won't leave just yet, will we?"

He rolled towards her, getting up to lean upon his elbow. "Certainly not! We have such a lovely hideaway here. And I shouldn't like to leave our friends."

This amused her. "How **is** George getting on?"

"Busy. Nowhere near saving enough to travel with us." He laughed softly, lying back upon his pillows.

"He's young. Likes to enjoy himself. I was the same at his age."

Mrs. Jackson hadn't known him at all when he was George's age, other than unsavory rumor. "I'm glad he's doing well."

"I'm going to suggest he buy property," Mr. Jackson said. "Something he can rent out. That'll help matters."

This seemed a good idea.

"He'd certainly be able to get a loan for it, either from the bank or his father."

Mr. Jackson went on like this for a while, as she lay watching him make plans for their next trip.

But that sounded a long way off.

Of course — as usual — her Mr. Jackson was right: Mr. Carlo knew the dangers here much better than either of them ever could.

"And I have something in mind," he said, which made her listen, "just in case." He turned just his head to face her. "Ever fancied a trip out West?"

She shrugged. "Never considered it."

He rolled towards her, going up on one elbow again, his face animated. "What if we bought **property** out that way? No one would ever imagine us going there!"

She considered it. "What sort of property?"

"What sort of property would you like?"

She gazed at the ceiling. "A big place. Somewhere we could grow a garden. With room for puppies to run. But something useful, that made the place we go to better." She looked over at him. "I wouldn't want to become a burden on anyone."

He nodded soberly. "That's a good idea." He lay upon his pillow, still facing her, his beautiful dark eyes wide. "A nice quiet place for us to retire."

She laughed softly. "Retire? What nonsense is this? You're only four and thirty!"

"We've no need to leave just yet." A wry smile lay upon his lips. "Which is fortunate, as I've just conceived the plan. It'd be many years before such a grand and lovely place might even be found, much less fashioned into what we wanted."

She snuggled into her pillow. "Good. Because for now, I'm quite fond of my life here."

<h1 style="text-align:center">22</h1>

As promised, Mr. Carlo's bill came sliding under the door shortly before dinner. After Mr. Jackson retrieved it, the couple peered at it together.

It seemed quite reasonable, with notation of "50% off for services rendered" above the total. A fair compromise, all things considered.

"Good grief," his wife exclaimed. "Have we spent **that** much? How will we **pay** for all this?"

He smiled at her. "Prices are overly high here, but the money here is much better than back home." He rested his arm upon her shoulders and kissed her forehead. "This is but a drop in one of many accounts."

She let out a breath. "I never imagined. However did you get all this money?"

"Sound investments, since I was little more than a boy. Never risking more than I could bear to lose, and making a great many friends of those who might help."

She stared at him in astonishment. "But —"

"But nothing. I've never taken a dime from anything criminal, except perhaps the inheritance I begged from my father. Back then, I had no idea what he was really up to. I was indeed the prodigal son, yet on returning home rich, I hardly received so much as a kind word." He sighed. "I suppose the circumstances made it difficult. But I wish we could have parted on better terms before he died."

His wife nodded.

"Have no fears about money, dear girl. We'd have to go through a lifetime of spending to match what I have now, even if not a penny more was added to it."

Her head rested upon his shoulder, and he felt her arm go round him. And he felt so grateful for his wife beside him, his friends, even for the little dog scratching at his leg to be walked. His life was very good.

***

Mr. Vienna and Mrs. Knight came that evening to dress the couple for dinner, and after checking on Bessie and her pups (who were all sleeping), the couple took the elevator down to the lobby.

As the couple approached the dining room, the Head Clerk, Mr. Francis. moved towards them. "Mr. Carlo asks if he might meet with you."

Mr. Jackson wasn't sure what to say. "Right now?"

"Yes, sir. He has dinner set up in the conference room."

"Oh," Mr. Jackson felt surprised. "Then of course."

Taking his wife's hand, he followed Mr. Francis to the door beside the front desk to the room they'd been questioned in the first morning they'd arrived here. But this time it had dinner set upon it, with platters set upon the sideboard and the young waiter he'd met a few days before standing by. "What an unexpected surprise!"

"It smells wonderful," his wife said.

After they'd eaten and Floyd had cleared everything away, Mr. Carlo came in.

Which Mr. Jackson thought odd. But he rose to shake the man's hand. "A pleasure to see you!"

"And you." Everyone seated, Mr. Carlo waved Floyd away. Once the young man left, he said, "So about our mutual little friend and her family: all is well."

Mr. Jackson said, "That's a relief."

"And about your question, Mrs. Jackson, I've asked around a bit. Russell wouldn't see me, but everyone else I've asked denies anything to do with it." He scoffed. "It's a silly thing to do, in front of a crowd like that."

True, Mr. Jackson thought. A back alley or poorly lit street corner seemed much more likely. "But something went on between Russell and Boyle, wouldn't you say?"

His wife nodded. "I forgot to tell you: I made some calls while you and Bessie were out on your walk. Apparently, Mr. Russell has started paying the tabloids for news articles about his men, to help his operation gain respectability."

Mr. Jackson stretched. "Seems strange to go to all that work if you're planning to kill a man."

"Well, sir, with your permission, your wife and I will learn the truth of all this." He turned to her. "Miss Franklin has agreed to meet tomorrow afternoon."

"That's fine," Mr. Jackson said. "I have some things to take care of tomorrow in any case."

"Very good," said Mr. Carlo. "Meet in front at two."

The couple returned to their parlor. To their surprise, Sergeant Nestor sat perfectly comfortably at their table.

"Good grief, Nestor," Mr. Jackson said. "What are you doing in here?"

"Well, I needed to speak with you. The front desk said you and Carlo were in a meeting. Since apparently I don't have the clout to get a desk clerk to interrupt said meeting, I found a maid to let me in. I figured you'd show up here sooner or later."

"And here we are," said Mr. Jackson, more than a little perturbed. "What do you want?"

"Don't be cross," he said cheerfully. "You've got to admit this is much nicer than the station. And I couldn't resist taking another peek at your puppies. I think we **will** take the dark brown one, when it's old enough." He gestured for them to move closer. "Please, sit down."

Glancing at his wife — who seemed merely amused at the situation rather than disturbed by it — they sat. Mr. Jackson said, "I presume you have some news?"

"If the one person who seems to know our dead man disappearing along with her mother is news."

Oh, dear, he thought. They'd completely forgotten to tell him.

Sergeant Nestor peered at them. "But I get the feeling this isn't news to you."

"Forgive us," Mrs. Jackson said. "We have news of our own. Miss Quinlan told us about Mr. Russell's involvement, and we feared for their safety."

The sergeant shrugged. "Everyone knows Russell owns the Mulder. The tough part is pinning anything on him."

Mr. Jackson leaned forward. "Miss Quinlan knows of meetings that went on with her Mr. Boyle and Mr. Russell, along with the names of some of Russell's men. Not sure if that'll help, but —"

"We know who they are," the sergeant said. "We know where they meet. I doubt she knows anything worth mentioning, and even if she did, I'd not like to put a speakeasy barmaid in front of a jury."

"Well," Mr. Jackson said, feeling a bit at sea, "the only other news is that a woman named Mabel Franklin could be involved."

Sergeant Nestor groaned, hand on his forehead.

Mrs. Jackson said, "So you know her."

"Yeah, we've met." The prospect of dealing with her seemed to daunt him. "The woman's got a whole cast of characters ready to give her an alibi at any moment. I'd have the phone in my hand with her dead on the slab in front of me and twenty gals would swear she was right there at their house." He shook his head. "Even if she didn't have half the mobsters in the city owing her, there's no way to convict." He looked at him. "Please don't tell me she did this."

"We don't think so," Mr. Jackson said. "But Mr. Carlo and my wife are going to meet with her tomorrow."

Sergeant Nestor raised his eyebrows. "Oh?" A laugh burst from him. "To be a fly on the wall at **that** meeting!"

Mr. Jackson felt quite amused.

His wife said, "Miss Quinlan saw Miss Franklin with Mr. Boyle earlier that evening. It's why Trixie slapped him. So it's very possible Miss Franklin saw the woman killed him."

"Hmm," said the sergeant. "And you think she'll tell you if she did?"

Mr. Jackson wondered that as well.

His wife hesitated, just a bit. "If I were to work as a ... what might one call it? Woman assassin? Then I'd want my pay. The very fact she was there with him in public meant she didn't plan to do the deed that night, but at some later date. So whoever did kill him just cost her a lot of money." Her face grew thoughtful. "As a matter of fact, she might be after our murderess too."

23

Sergeant Nestor leaned forward. "Then we have to find this woman before Mabel Franklin does. I want her arrested, not dead in the street!"

"We'll do our best," Mr. Jackson said. "But if Miss Franklin gets the idea we're working with you, she won't tell my wife a thing."

"You have a point," the sergeant said. "I'll stay away from now on."

Good, Mr. Jackson thought, still annoyed at the man's intrusion. "Anything else we should know?"

"I learned more about the man Boyle embezzled from," Sergeant Nestor said. "But I'm afraid that turned out to be a dead end."

"What do you mean?"

"Victor Hoffmann had put his — and his family's — life savings into the company. The theft ruined them all. The company had to liquidate. The man went into bankruptcy. The cost of the trial threw his family into poverty. I tracked down his assistant, who now works at a local jeweler. He told me Mr. Hoffmann was despondent, particularly as the trial dragged on and the bills began to pile up. Mr. Hoffmann's no suspect: he took his own life before Boyle ever saw a day of prison."

Mrs. Jackson gasped.

Sergeant Nestor nodded. "His parents are alive, but have alibis for the evening. He has a younger sister named Pauline, but she married and moved away some time ago. There seems to be bad blood between them: I don't think the parents approved of her husband."

Mr. Jackson said, "Did you happen to ask as to the sister's married name? Or where she moved to?"

"She lives in Oak Lawn now. She wasn't home when I called on them, but I spoke with her husband, a Mr. Milton Shapiro." The sergeant shrugged. "Perfectly respectable businessman. He swears she was at home with him on New Years' Eve."

Mr. Jackson felt close to the answer. "That phone number on the notepad — who was Boyle going to call?"

"No one's answering the number, and the address is an abandoned building. But we found some cigarette butts which looked recent."

Another mystery.

His wife said, "What about the bullet? I presume you found the shell casing."

"Yep," Sergeant Nestor said. "A twenty-five caliber automatic Colt pistol cartridge. You can buy them anywhere. The particular gun it was used in hasn't been involved in any other crimes."

Mr. Jackson said, "What about Mr. D'Angelo? He claimed he'd never seen Mr. Boyle before then. But I've found two people already who saw him there each of the two nights earlier."

"Who?"

Mr. Jackson said, "A waitress, as well as one of the band members."

His wife leaned forward. "That bartender has to know something. What else did you learn about him?"

Sergeant Nestor said, "My man that brought the bartender home said Mr. D'Angelo lived by himself in a one-room apartment."

"That sounds very much like poor Trixie," his wife said quietly.

"He pays his rent, keeps to himself, doesn't cause trouble." Sergeant Nestor looked uncertain. "I've had him in for questioning once already. I'm concerned we might lose our killer if he starts thinking we suspect him and calls her."

"But —"

"I've got men on him," the sergeant said. "He's not going anywhere."

They were missing something, of that Mr. Jackson felt certain. But what? "There had to be a reason Mr. Boyle suddenly stopped going to his speakeasy." He turned to his wife. "Perhaps your meeting with Miss Franklin tomorrow will bring us at the very least, that answer."

24

They met her outside a stylish bistro in the Loop. Tall, willowy, brown-haired, with an angular face. Her high-fashion red woolen dress hung from her slender body in just the right way, this year's wide-brimmed hat angled perfectly on her head.

Miss Mabel Franklin wasn't exactly unattractive, Mrs. Jackson thought. It was just that she didn't care if anyone in the world thought so.

A certain kind of man found that tremendously appealing.

Mr. Carlo was clearly that kind of man. He seemed changed in her presence: tongue-tied, almost shy.

Mabel Franklin came close to ignoring him.

"So it is really you," she said to Mrs. Jackson. "The queen of the South here, in the flesh!" She grasped Mrs. Jackson's hand with black silken gloves which went to her elbow (presumably better when shooting someone), her eyes positively aglow. "And you're really here!"

Mrs. Jackson found this amusing. "In the flesh."

They moved inside, to a table apparently kept open just for her. "Please," Miss Franklin said, "sit down." After they sat, she said, "What can I do for you?"

"Mark Boyle. Why were you going to kill him?"

"Oh, I don't know. I never ask, and they never tell."

A wistful look came over the woman's face. "The one who got away." She let out a small, bitter laugh. "I could've used the money. A thousand dollars gone," she snapped the fingers of her right hand, "just like that."

"So you don't know why he was there instead of at the Mulder."

She shrugged, shaking her head.

Mr. Carlo sounded upset. "This woman's ruining my business! I'll pay you that much right now if you let me take care of this myself."

Without so much as looking his way, Miss Franklin held out a gloved hand. After fumbling a bit, Mr. Carlo deposited a thick wad into it.

Did they have to worry about **him** now, too?

Mrs. Jackson leaned forward. "You haven't made a name for yourself by being stupid. So I know you weren't planning on killing him that night." She leaned back. "Tell me what happened."

Miss Franklin rolled her eyes, giving an impatient sigh. "He asked me to dinner. We'd just been there two nights before, so I knew the place. We get seated at a table, order drinks. We'd been there a while, had a couple of drinks. Suddenly, he gets up, goes over to this ... child, really. A pretty little thing, but much too young to be there. They argue, she slaps him. When I ask what's going on, he won't answer. So I go freshen up. The place was crowded already: there was quite a line. When I get back, this brown-haired tart was all over him! I told him you can't be doing this: you gotta pick. He told me if I didn't like it to leave." She shrugged. "So I did. Me and my girls went to a movie."

"Tell me about the girl," Mrs. Jackson said.

"Hmm ... about my height. Brown eyes ..."

"Left-handed?"

Miss Franklin considered this for a moment. "Yes, I do believe so."

That had to be his killer. "What was she wearing?"

"A black sequined dress." She sighed. "A pity you're going to kill her. She has style."

25

While Mrs. Jackson was otherwise occupied, Mr. Jackson and several of the maids carefully transported the puppies in their blanket — supported by a large tray — down the elevator to the veterinary's. Bessie followed closely behind.

That accomplished, he and George Neuberg went to the fitness club. They played several rousing games of tennis, then sat in the sauna.

Few men were there at this time of day. So they reclined in a sunny corner, completely to themselves other than the occasional waiter, sipping iced tea.

George said, "Might I ask something?"

"Of course," Mr. Jackson said.

"You tell me that you're involved with not only finding a murderess, but keeping an assassin from finding her first."

Mr. Jackson laughed. "Yes, well said."

"But why? Why are you doing this?"

He considered this for a moment. "When I was a boy, someone I very much cared about was murdered."

George gaped at him.

"I tried for years to learn why he was killed, but never did." At this, he felt more than a bit melancholy. "Perhaps in this case, I can." He shrugged. "Or perhaps not. But what I really mean to say is ... if I were killed, I'd want someone to care enough to find out why."

George grasped his hand tightly for a moment, then gave it a couple of short pats. "I know you'll succeed: I can feel it."

Mr. Jackson felt his spirits quite renewed, "I'm grateful to hear it. Right now, I feel at a loss."

"If there's any way I can help —"

"Certainly I'll let you know." He sipped at his iced tea. "Do you think you'd ever like to go out West?"

George shrugged. "Never even considered it."

"Well, my wife and I love it here, every bit. But sooner or later —"

"You'll have to move on. I get it." He fell silent for a while. "And you want me to go with you."

"Sure. Why not?"

"Where, out West?"

"Oh, I don't know." He chuckled to himself. "I haven't even talked to my men about it yet." He put the tall glass on the little table between them. "I was just thinking of the future."

George smiled to himself. "That's very kind of you. And in theory, of course I'd want to tag along. But I couldn't possibly say one way or the other until I knew the details."

"Fair enough." For now, it was only a thought, an idea of a definite place that was all their own. "What kind of place would you like?"

George put his hands behind his head, gazing at the ceiling. "Some place busy, full of people and things to do. Cosmopolitan, if you will."

There was one such place that came to mind. But would they be able to have land in that big city where puppies could run? What if he couldn't find a place with what everyone wanted in one spot?

George laughed, turning his head towards him. "Don't mind me. If you gotta choose, go with what your wife wants. From what my Pa tells me, that makes everyone happier."

***

On the way back to the Hotel, Mrs. Jackson stopped by Ophelia's boarding house. Mrs. Kilpatrick, a dumpy old lady of perhaps seventy, opened the door. "Oh, yeah, she's here. Come on in and I'll fetch her."

Leaving Mrs. Jackson in the front hall, she yelled up, "Ophelia! There's some lady to see you!"

Ophelia Denton came running down the narrow wooden stair in a day dress and stockinged feet, then stopped when she saw her. "Oh!"

Mrs. Jackson almost laughed. "May I come up, or would you like to go for a walk?"

By this time, every door was open, as girls peeked out to see the commotion.

Ophelia blushed. "You can come up if you like."

So Mrs. Jackson went up the creaking staircase to Ophelia's room. One room, with posters, dried flowers, bits of dance card, portraits, ticket stubs, and other memorabilia covering the walls. A narrow closet hung open, holding various dresses, with three pairs of shoes at the bottom. The bed was unmade and stockings lay upon the floor.

"Oh!" The girl rushed to move aside the mess and cover the bed. "Want to sit down?"

A narrow bit of table was pushed up against one wall with two chairs. Mrs. Jackson selected one. "Here is perfectly fine."

Ophelia plopped herself upon the other. "If I knew you were coming, I would've cleaned up."

"Don't fret yourself," Mrs. Jackson said. "How are you? I thought I'd stop by."

Ophelia gave a one-shoulder shrug. "I have to work tonight."

"A pity."

The girl let out a short laugh. "Not really; it pays the rent." That seemed to spark some memory, because her face changed, became bold. "No, I like my job just fine."

Mrs. Jackson smiled to herself. "It's good to be doing what you love."

"Are you feeling all right?"

Mrs. Jackson nodded. "I still have a bit of a cough, but it's not nearly so bad as it was."

Ophelia lowered her voice. "Did you really go see that awful woman?"

"I did! She was actually very nice." Mrs. Jackson related the conversation they'd had. "I thought it was funny, seeing Mr. Carlo like that."

"But ..." Ophelia leaned forward to speak at a whisper. "Aren't you scared she's gonna tell someone who you are?"

"Her? Not at all. I mean, I don't know for sure! But just think of it. Any of the mobsters she tells either won't care or be glad I got out. Less competition for them."

Ophelia's face grew thoughtful. "Oh ..."

"And if she went to the Feds, well, that'd be the end of her career!"

"But shouldn't you tell the police you met her?"

"I already did. Before I even went. They know her, but they can't put her in jail. They don't have any proof."

"That's not right," Ophelia said. "For her to just get away with doing stuff like that."

Mrs. Jackson let out a sigh. "I know. But sooner or later, she'll make a mistake. And then she'll get caught. Criminals always do."

26

W hen Mrs. Jackson returned to the Myriad Hotel, Bessie came running out to greet her.

Mr. Jackson had tea and sandwiches set up for them in the parlor. He sat at the small tea-table near the window reading the news. "Ah, there you are!"

She kissed his cheek and sat across from him at the tea-table. "Did you and George have fun?"

"We most certainly did." He closed the paper, set it down. "Learn anything interesting?"

"Well, as a matter of fact, yes. Mark Boyle had invited Mabel Franklin to dinner. And guess what? They'd been there two nights earlier."

Mr. Jackson nodded. "The three women were actually just two."

"Yes! And like Trixie said, Miss Franklin saw the girl slap Mr. Boyle. But then a tall, left-handed, brown-haired woman wearing a black sequined dress forced herself into the scene while Miss Franklin was in the powder room. When Miss Franklin returned, there was an argument —"

"Naturally."

"And Miss Franklin left." She leaned forward. "Mr. Carlo has paid her the money she lost in order to, and I quote, 'take care of this myself'."

"So now we have Carlo to worry about."

"Yes." She got up, went to the food, got some of the small sandwiches and some tea, and returned to her chair. "Other than that, well, she didn't know why they wanted the man dead, or why he'd prefer to meet at Carlo's place rather than Russell's." She shrugged. "Apparently they just tell her who and she does the job."

Mr. Jackson nodded. "And since she didn't do it, she hasn't told you anything to implicate herself in anything else." He sipped at his cup, which from the smell of it, was coffee. "Smart."

"She is, very much so. I wonder how she got into such a life."

"Well," Mr. Jackson said, "I don't suppose that's something we'll ever know."

"Did you ever get a chance to meet with Harry's neighbor?"

"As a matter of fact, I did: they were out front when I arrived from the fitness club." He hesitated. "I don't know if it's even worth mentioning."

She could tell by his face the encounter hadn't been a pleasant one. "Oh, dear. What happened?"

He let out a breath. "Unpleasant young European fellow with a terrible thick accent." An ironic laugh burst from him. "If he would've been the remotest bit polite, we could've just conversed in German."

This amused her: he knew more languages than anyone she'd ever met. "Oh, you scoundrel: you let the poor man struggle!"

"Hmph," he said, sounding more than a bit annoyed. "He deserved it." He shook his head. "He wouldn't even look at me, and only would speak to Harry. As if I weren't even there!"

She sighed, taking his hand. "I'm sorry."

"He told us much the same as you did. But then he said something interesting. Right before midnight, the young woman took something from the man's pocket."

"His wallet?" Could this have been a robbery? But only the wallet was gone: his money hadn't been taken.

"I thought perhaps instead she might have taken the lighter. We never found it. But then the man had very little on him, so who knows?" He held his cup midair, face thoughtful. "There is one way to perhaps learn what's going on at the Mulder, though."

"Surely you don't mean —"

"Yes, dear girl. George doesn't work tonight." He set his cup down, giving her a broad smile. "I think I'll take him out on the town."

27

It took a bit of doing for Mr. Jackson to get the codes for entrance into the Mulder. Fortunately, the place only changed the codes once a month, and Trixie Quinlan was able to provide them.

The girl's aunt's home was smallish on the inside, but with plenty of room out back. She had four sons, and the sounds of them tumbling around outside in the twilight echoed through the hallway as Miss Trixie told them the information.

As Mr. Jackson and Mr. Carlo returned to the Hotel, Mr. Carlo said, "Now, you're just there to look. There could be any number of reasons Boyle didn't want to drink there. So try to stay out of trouble."

Mr. Jackson thought this quite amusing. "Trouble? Me? I am the very soul of discretion." It was likely he wouldn't discover anything at all. But if something was wrong, he felt sure he could sniff it out.

"Well, good luck," Mr. Carlo said. "You're not going alone, are you?"

"No, not at all — I'm bringing a friend along."

Mr. Carlo nodded. "Good."

Mr. Jackson felt relieved that Carlo hadn't asked who would accompany him. Strictly speaking, George wasn't supposed to fraternize with the guests like this. But what Mr. Carlo didn't know wouldn't hurt him.

The Mulder was, on the face of it, a little hole-in-the-wall restaurant on the South Side, with "the best pizza in town". But when Mr. Jackson asked for a double burger with Worcestershire sauce and a ginger ale float, the man led them to a door and down a winding stair.

Mr. Jackson turned to George. "Pretty fun, eh?"

The man at the door below was lit by a single bulb overhead. "Need anything else?"

Miss Trixie had said they'd say this to you if they thought you might be a cop. Mr. Jackson grinned at the man. "A million bucks would help."

The men tensed up.

"But a blue garter works just fine."

Both the men laughed. The man who'd led them downstairs said, "You're all right, Mister." Opening the door, the second man gestured for them to enter.

Between the Myriad Hotel's speakeasy and Club Patruni (where Miss Ophelia Denton danced), this lay in-between in size and capacity. A band played up front, and a woman sang. It was only half-full this early on a Friday night, and they were led past the bar to a smallish table off to one side.

Mr. Jackson tried not to stare at the waitresses: their skirts went up past their knees!

"Heh," George said. "A leg man, are you?"

"I never considered it." He felt his cheeks burn. "I suppose I am." He'd never had a second glance at any woman other than his wife before.

Then he smiled to himself. His wife was lovely, at home, and waiting for his return. Hopefully they'd find out what they needed to know here quickly, so he might get back to her.

A waiter wearing a full apron came by. "What'll you have, sirs?"

"Whiskey sour for me," said George.

Mr. Jackson said, "Whatever you've got on tap."

"Coming right up."

A companionable silence fell. Mr. Jackson surveyed the room. The staff seemed happy. The customers conversed in a relaxed manner, and drank without ill effect. What could possibly be going on? "Do you see anything at all odd here?"

"Nope."

Mr. Jackson felt pleased with the evening so far. With the promotion to Headwaiter, he and George didn't get to spend nearly as much time with each other as they used to. But once George had some men trained up, he'd have more time off.

George said, "I thought you didn't drink."

"I'm not sure if my grandfather was that religious, or if he just thought it unsafe, but he forbade any kind of alcohol on his property. So I never got the taste for it. But I didn't think it wise to stand out by not ordering." Mr. Jackson shrugged. "No one says I have to drink it."

George laughed. "Right you are."

The bartender didn't seem to be making anything. Rather, he stood there talking to the waiter.

George sighed. "I wish they'd hurry up; I'm thirsty."

"Don't be in such a rush," said Mr. Jackson, but privately, he agreed. What could they possibly be discussing?

Just then, every door in the place — some he hadn't even noticed — opened up, and dozens of men wearing suits streamed in, holding guns. One called out, "This is a Federal raid!"

Mr. Jackson sat there, for the first time in a while struck silent with terror. This was a scene from his worst nightmares.

The Feds had caught him.

28

The Agents began grabbing customers, barmaids, waiters, dragging them out.

Mr. Jackson's mind raced.

Had they actually done anything illegal? He didn't know. If they pressed charges, though, started to dig deeper, then they might learn about his wife.

He couldn't have that happen.

What could he do? What should he say?

Then an answer came to him.

It wasn't ideal by any means. But if they got the right sort of men questioning them, it might work. "George, say nothing. Not even a word. If they insist, tell them you won't answer without me present."

"But —"

"Do you trust me?"

The men moved from table to table, getting closer.

George nodded.

"Even if I might say or do something that harms your reputation?"

Their eyes met. "I trust you with my life," George said. "Do what you must."

Mr. Jackson and George were frisked, put into a truck, then taken to a Federal holding area with everyone else in the bar, including the women. They all sat in a large, grimy cell for some time.

And he worried.

If my idea doesn't work, what then?

Calm yourself, he thought. You have lawyers. Better yet, you're married. You can't be forced to testify against her. You can't even be forced to give her real name.

Unless they saw the flier, they might not even realize who she was.

But if he did get out of this mess tonight, though, home and safe ... what should he do?

Should he take his wife and leave?

No, he decided. She'd be heartbroken, terrified, yet again wrenched from what had become home and family. To do this to her twice in one year ... it seemed inconceivable.

I'll wait, he thought. See how this plays out. She doesn't need to know.

Eventually, Hector Jackson and George Neuberg were put across a table from two stern-looking men. The men sat far from each other, yet kept glancing at each other, and at George.

My lovely George, Mr. Jackson thought, feeling a bit more hope with each glance the two men made. *This just might work.*

A third man stood at the door behind them, presumably to intimidate them, to block the door in case they might run, or perhaps both. Mr. Jackson had seen these tactics before, but he hoped George wasn't too unnerved by it all.

So far, no one had spoken.

Perhaps these Feds thought the two would become daunted by the silence and tell everything. Now he felt glad he'd warned George to say nothing.

Finally, the man Mr. Jackson had pegged as the leader spoke. "I'm Special Agent Andrew Chapman," he gestured to the man beside him. "This is Special Agent Claude Haley," he gestured at the man at the door, "and that is Special Agent Fred Scott. Do you know why you're here?"

Mr. Jackson shrugged, heart pounding. "I presume it's illegal to sit in a speakeasy."

Agent Chapman frowned. "Not exactly." He glanced at George.

"Well, since we'd only just arrived," Mr. Jackson said, "then I can't imagine why we're here."

"You know," Agent Chapman said, recovering his composure, "I can't imagine why you **were** there. A rich businessman staying at one of the premier hotels in Chicago along with the same hotel's Headwaiter, in some dingy speakeasy on the South Side?"

"I'm impressed," said Mr. Jackson. "So I'll tell you why we were there." With that, he told them about the murder in the Myriad Hotel, the current facts of the matter, and how curiosity about what could possibly be going on at the Mulder brought them there to see for themselves. "Sergeant Benjamin Nestor of the Chicago Police Department can corroborate all this."

Agent Chapman nodded to Agent Scott, who left, locking the door behind him. Then he leaned his elbows on the table. "So you're assisting in a murder investigation? Why?"

"Well, the owner of the hotel asked me to. I've assisted him before."

"I see." It was fairly obvious that the man did not. "Mr. Carlo." He scoffed. "We've heard of him."

Mr. Jackson nodded.

"Well, we'll talk with this Sergeant Nestor, then we'll decide what to do with you." Then he glanced over at George. "You need anything?"

Mr. Jackson put his hand on George's. "We'd appreciate it if we might be kept in the same room. We're such very good pals, you see."

"Ugh!" The Agents looked appalled, drawing back.

Agent Chapman stood, obviously annoyed. "All right; we're done here. Both of you clowns, out!"

On the sidewalk outside, Mr. Jackson and George looked at each other for a moment, then broke down laughing. "The look on his face," George said. "That was inspired."

Mr. Jackson couldn't stop laughing until they'd flagged down a taxi, collapsing into it. "Oh, goodness." He wiped a tear from his eye. "This has been the most fun I've had in a very long time."

29

When Mr. Jackson arrived back at the Hotel to a cheerful, sleepy wife and her happy little dogs, he didn't mention anything to her about the Feds. "It seemed like a perfectly ordinary bar. I'm not sure at all why Mr. Boyle feared to go there."

Satisfied, his wife went peacefully back to bed. He didn't fall asleep for some time.

The next morning, as the sky was just beginning to pale, Mr. Jackson sat up in bed, brooding. This wasn't over yet.

The Feds knew where he and George were. If they should inquire further ....

Just wait, he told himself. Making any sudden moves now would only make them suspicious.

He took a deep breath, let it out. No sense worrying over something that might not even happen.

His wife opened her eyes, turning to him with a smile. "You're up early."

He smiled at her. "I suppose I am. Did you rest well?"

"I did." She got up on an elbow. "You look worried. Is anything wrong?"

He shook his head, leaned over to kiss her forehead. He hated lying to her. But what might he say of the truth? "I wish now that we hadn't gone to the Mulder. If we should have to do more investigation, well, now they know our faces."

She nodded, lips pursed, then sat up, hugging her knees. "Well if so, we can ask the sergeant to send his own men there next time."

Mr. Jackson let out an amused laugh. "I can just imagine his budget officer's face on that regard. From the sound of it, the Chicago Police Department barely has enough men to respond to the crime scenes, much less do much about them."

After his wife had left and before Mr. Vienna was to arrive, Sergeant Nestor knocked at their parlor door. The man looked none too pleased. "What possessed you to go to the Mulder, of all places, alone?"

"George Neuberg was with me," Mr. Jackson said.

Sergeant Nestor scowled. "Ugh." He stormed into the room. "You're lucky the both of you are still alive."

That seemed odd. "Here, sit down." Once the sergeant had seated himself at the rosewood table, Mr. Jackson said, "Why do you say that? What's wrong?"

"You know why the Feds are interested in the Mulder? Because it's been the center of a bad liquor operation. Dozens of people have died so far."

"Oh." Mr. Jackson felt chagrined. "Good thing neither of us had a chance to drink."

The sergeant let out a short laugh. "They'd not stay around long if they began poisoning their own customers. But they've sold bad liquor to smaller operations to try to drive them out of business. If they'd learned you were with Carlo, they might have killed you both, thinking you to be his spies."

"Whew." They'd been very lucky. "I had no idea."

Sergeant Nestor scoffed. "The Agent I spoke with last night quizzed me for almost an hour about what I might know about it." He laughed then. "Whatever you did to get them to throw you out must have really angered him. He ranted about 'those upstart young men' for a full twenty minutes."

"Heh," Mr. Jackson said. "Fortunately, I found myself in front of two gentlemen who had yet to admit to their true hearts' desires. Naturally, I took advantage."

The sergeant raised an eyebrow. "I have no idea what you're talking about."

"Never you mind." Since the Agents thought he and George were together, they evidently never even considered that he might also have a wife. And suddenly, in a flash, Mr. Jackson realized something. "The phone number. Boyle had gone to the Feds!"

"Yes!" The sergeant sounded impressed. "And when he disappeared, they felt forced to raid the Mulder before Russell destroyed the evidence."

"Did he? I mean, did they find anything?"

The sergeant shrugged. "If so, they didn't tell me."

"Please don't say anything to my wife about the Feds. She's under enough strain as it is."

Sergeant Nestor nodded soberly.

Mr. Jackson let out a relieved breath. "So what are we going to do about Ralph D'Angelo, the bartender? Mr. Carlo has said some things that make my wife and I think he's going to take matters into his own hands."

"Well, that's more than a little concerning," the sergeant said. He sat quietly for a moment. "I'll have my men put Mr. D'Angelo into protective custody. Come down to the station too if you like. Maybe this guy needs a different approach, and I think you can help."

30

When his wife returned from helping Monsieur with his rooftop gardens, when they'd been dressed for breakfast and their retainers had left, Mr. Jackson told her about Sergeant Nestor's visit. Of course, he left out the part about the Feds.

She seemed both surprised and confused. "So why was he here in the first place?"

"He heard that we went to the Mulder and was worried for us. This Mr. Russell sounds like the worst sort of man."

"I suppose." She had a slight frown. "I also called on Miss Trixie Quinlan at her aunt's house. That is to say, I telephoned. It must have been just after you left there. The missing wallet bothered me. What I learned was that he never carried one."

"Strange, although not all men do."

"Something's going on that I don't understand. If the killer did take the lighter, why?" Her frown grew deeper. "And the sergeant wants us to go to the police station right now ... why?"

He put a hand on her shoulder. "Trust me: it's nothing bad. He's worried about Carlo going after the bartender, and thinks that together, we might be able to persuade Mr. D'Angelo to talk."

His wife shook her head. "Something's not right."

"You're welcome to stay here if you prefer."

"No. It's not that." She took a deep breath, peering at him. "Are you lying to me?"

For some reason, he felt moved. "Come sit closer."

So they sat beside each other on the sofa, and he wrapped his arms around her.

"Everything I've told you is true." How could he possibly say this? "But I left something out." He remembered how she reacted when they first arrived to even a hint of this, and he pulled her close. "You must promise not to be afraid. I would not lie to you in this: we are safe, and all is entirely well."

She looked up at him, eyes huge. "I trust you. But only if you tell me everything."

That made him smile. "When George and I went to the Mulder, we'd not been there ten minutes before the Feds arrived."

She gasped. "No."

"Oh, goodness, yes. Dozens of them. I felt terrified." With that, he told her the entire story: being dragged away, the long, frightening hours in the holding cell.

But then he told her about meeting the three Agents, and the way he and George tricked them. By the end, they were both laughing, with tears in their eyes.

He took her face in his hands. "I never wanted to lie to you. But you looked so happy when I came home. You slept so peacefully. I ... I didn't want to cause you more grief and fear." He took her hands. "You've gone through too much already."

She nodded slowly, her eyes upon his. "Thank you for telling me." She sighed, head downcast. "I understand so many things now, things I wish I would have before." Then she smiled. "If the sergeant thinks we can help in some way, then I'll be happy to."

***

So after breakfast, Mr and Mrs. Jackson went down to the police station.

Mr. Ralph D'Angelo sat quietly in the holding room, clearly curious as to what had happened. "Do I need a lawyer?"

"Eventually, yes, you might," Sergeant Nestor said. "But right now, I'm more concerned about your safety." He leaned forward. "I think you know who killed that man. You were right there. I don't care how busy you were; you had to have seen at least some of what went on." Sergeant Nestor sat across the table from him. "Now, I don't know if you are trying to protect this woman because you care about her, or you're trying to protect her because you're in on it." He held up a hand at the man's protest. "But there's something you might not know: there's an assassin after her —"

The bartender seemed to notice the couple at that point. When he glanced at them, they both nodded.

Mr. D'Angelo's face turned a remarkable shade of greenish pale.

"- and we have to find her before they do. Or before Mr. Carlo or his men find you and decide to beat her name out of you." Sergeant Nestor leaned back. "That's why you're here: to keep you alive." He took a deep breath. "If you help us find her, you won't be charged with anything at all. You have my word."

The man hunched over the table, hands clasped together in front of him, and was silent for some time. "Okay," he finally said. "Yeah, I know her." He shut his eyes tightly. "She used to be my wife."

31

Mr. Jackson stared at the man. He found himself sitting beside the sergeant. "What happened?"

Mr. D'Angelo sighed, running his hands through his hair. "We married at sixteen, for love. Her parents didn't like it, but they let us live with them. Her parents became like parents to me. And I persuaded them to risk everything we had on an investment." He took a deep breath. "We lost it all. Then things got even worse." His eyes shut, and his lashes grew moist.

After a moment, he opened his eyes. "We had barely a thing to eat. The utilities turned off our lights, then our heat. We'd go out, me and my wife, to find sticks for the fireplace so we didn't freeze." His face twisted in anguish. "But then I learned her parents had sold their wedding rings to pay the mortgage." He let his hands drop to the table. "It was more than I could take! So I pretended I had a gun, and —"

"Robbed the grocery," Sergeant Nestor said.

Mr. Jackson felt his wife's hand on his shoulder, and he grasped it, feeling bleak.

Mr. D'Angelo shook his head, still staring at the table. "It only ended with me in prison. She divorced me, her family disowned me." He shrugged. "I'm not sure which hurts more."

They fell quiet for a moment.

"Mr. D'Angelo," the sergeant said. "What's your wife's name? We're very concerned for her safety. We have to find her before these people do."

He glanced at all of them. "She got remarried. Her name's Pauline Shapiro."

Sergeant Nestor rose. "Her husband lied to me! I'm going to go drag both of them in, right now."

"Wait." Mr. Jackson sat gazing at the bartender for a moment. If someone was watching the station. If someone knew Mr. D'Angelo was here. If anyone had followed him and his wife there ... this could turn ugly, fast. "I think I know a safer way for us all."

32

With each day's passing, Milton Shapiro felt more and more uneasy.

The police had come to their door asking where his wife had been on New Year's Eve. Of course, he'd said she was with him: it was his duty to protect her.

But she hadn't been there. She hadn't been home until close to dawn.

She'd said she was going out with her friends. She was young, and pretty, and of course he let her go. It wasn't fair to keep a young woman from enjoying herself. When he asked her about it after the police left, she swore she'd been with her friends.

But now he wasn't so sure.

His mother had told him it was a mistake to marry a so much younger woman. "She'll find a young man and you'll be paying alimony, just you wait and see."

But this wasn't about where she'd been or who she'd been with anymore. They said a man was murdered.

Pauline refused to speak of it. But with each day that passed, she became more relaxed, almost happy. She wasn't even using the sleeping powder the doctor prescribed for her anymore.

And for some reason, it worried him.

So when the phone rang, he almost jumped from his chair, thinking it was the police come at last.

Instead, a deep, rich, soothing voice spoke: "This is Mr. Hector Jackson from KWY Radio in Chicago. Is this the home of Mrs. Pauline Shapiro?"

"It is. May I ask what this is about?"

"Certainly, sir. Do I have the pleasure of speaking with her husband?"

The man's voice was so impressive, well, he just had to answer. "Why, yes! I'm her husband."

Pauline poked her head around the corner. "What's going on?"

Milton gestured frantically for her to come close by, so she might hear, too. "My wife's on the line."

"Congratulations," Mr. Jackson said, "from KWY Radio in Chicago. You've won a brand new automobile!"

Milton felt stunned. "We have?"

He and his wife stared at each other. She said, "How did I win a car?"

"Well, ma'am," Mr. Jackson said, "if you didn't enter into the drawing, then someone must have put your name in."

Pauline looked flabbergasted. "I suppose so!"

"Congratulations, my dear. You've won a brand new 1922 Pierce Arrow Coupe, tax and license paid, with fuel for a year. A magnificent luxury vehicle, indeed! Now, all that's needed is for you and your husband to come to the Chicago Civic Auditorium at 3 P.M. tomorrow to pick it up. Make sure to bring your identification!"

Milton thought this sounded too good to be true. "When did this contest happen?"

"Oh, we've been having the drawing for weeks now," Mr. Jackson said. "To celebrate the inaugural season of KWY Radio in Chicago. You're the envy of the city!"

Milton got out a notepad and a pen. "You say your name is Jackson?"

"Yes, sir, Mr. Hector Jackson from KWY Radio, Chicago. I will tell you, sir, that the station is quite pleased a winner is coming all the way from Oak Lawn! A nice expansion of their audience, I must say."

"Yes, yes," Milton said distractedly, "of course. And 3 P.M. at the Chicago Civic Auditorium."

"Yes, sir. Would you like directions?"

"No, no," Milton said. "I know where it is."

"Splendid. It'll be a lovely day: a buffet, a few speeches from our director, and of course, the Pierce Arrow Coupe! You do drive, I take it?"

"Well, yes." They had a Model T. Perfectly respectable, to be sure, but nothing at all like what this man had described.

"Wonderful. Mr and Mrs. Shapiro, we are really looking forward to meeting you."

Milton hung up the phone. He and his wife stared at each other.

Her face burst into smiles, and she flung her hands into the air. "Woo hoo!"

"Don't get too excited," Milton said. "This sounds like some kind of swindle." He picked up the receiver. "Connect me to KWY Radio, Chicago."

He called KWY Radio, he even called the Chicago Civic Auditorium. They agreed: didn't Mr. Hector

Jackson have a marvelous voice? And yes, they were indeed giving away a car tomorrow.

So the next afternoon, Milton and his wife, excited and nervous both, got into their Sunday best and made the trip into downtown Chicago.

When they reached the Civic Auditorium, balloons and streamers festooned the front. A valet took their car. A beautiful woman with light brown skin, blue eyes, and bobbed black hair put a enormous bouquet into his wife's arms. "Congratulations!"

Milton could only gape at the spectacle. Attendants opened the doors.

Cheers erupted. Smiling faces were all around. Music poured forth. Mr. Jackson's voice came from overhead. A host of dressed-up couples mingled inside holding champagne glasses.

In the lobby stood a sparkling new auto!

Milton was surprised speechless. This was real!

Just then, an older man in street clothes stood beside him. "Mrs. Pauline Shapiro?"

Milton turned to his wife, who had a dazed look on her face. She focused on the older man. "Why, yes!"

The man, for some reason, looked sad. "I'm Sergeant Benjamin Nestor. You're under arrest for the murder of Mark Boyle."

33

Mr. Jackson switched off the microphone and turned to George Neuberg. "Tell your father thanks for loaning us the car."

George laughed. "He's gonna love this story."

In Mrs. Shapiro's purse lay a pearl-handled gun and a cast iron Pist-o-liter with a piece chipped off of the handle, both of which were taken from her by forensics men before the police proceeded further.

The couple rode with Sergeant Nestor down to the police station, and were allowed to watch — safely behind glass — as Milton and Pauline Shapiro were questioned. Or rather, as the two of them argued — both with each other and the lawyer Milton Shapiro had immediately called in.

Mr. D'Angelo sat in the corner, having been cautioned by the Sergeant not to say a word, no matter how his former wife might provoke him.

Pauline blurted out, "I don't deny any of it!"

"Mrs. Shapiro," the lawyer said, "I must urge you —"

"Oh, can it," she snapped. "He killed my brother. So I killed him."

"But sweetheart," Mr. Shapiro said. "He wasn't responsible for your brother's death!"

"Wait," Sergeant Nestor said, notebook open. "Please, all of you. Start from the beginning. We know your brother lost his business after Mr. Boyle stole his entire receipts from him. We know that during the trial, he took his life."

Pauline began to cry.

"But what we don't know is how you ended up here. Can you tell us anything more?" The sergeant turned to Pauline's lawyer. "She's already confessed. It'd help later on if she cooperates."

"I don't care what you do to me," she sobbed. "Victor was my brother! He'd been saving to start his business ever since I was a little girl. We gave him whatever his business needed. My husband and I, our parents, that man ruined us all. Ralph wouldn't have gone to jail if not for him."

"But you left him when he did," the sergeant said.

"Yeah, I left him," Pauline said. "My parents wanted me to. They had set me up with Milton here." She glanced at him. "No offense, darling, but you had money and they were dead broke." She sighed, giving Mr. D'Angelo a quick glance. "I don't think Ralph ever forgave me for it, though."

On the other side of the glass, Mr. Jackson murmured, "On the contrary: I think Mr. D'Angelo still loves her."

Mr. Shapiro looked devastated; Mr. Jackson felt sorry for the man.

She continued, "I saw an article about Boyle in some tabloid. And it made me so angry! Here he was getting praised, with a new name and reputation, while my brother lay dead. And it also scared me."

"Scared you?" Sergeant Nestor sounded confused. "Why?"

"That guy threatened to kill all of us — my parents, everyone — if my brother pressed charges. Seeing him there out free like that made me scared he'd come kill us." She clasped her hands together so tightly her fingers went bright pink, her knuckles white. "That was when I decided to do it. Kill him. Before he got to us."

Sergeant Nestor sounded tired, like he'd heard this story too many times before. "So what happened then?"

"I called the tabloid, said I was calling for my boss who wanted to do an interview and did they have his information? They gave me his address and everything. After that I started checking up on him. He was with some mobster, running around with booze, women ... that made me even more sure I was doing the right thing. My Ma and Pa, Ralph ... they might hate me now, but I couldn't let Boyle kill them. And to see him out happy ... it was unfair."

Mr. Shapiro said, "Didn't he do his time, though? In prison? Wasn't that enough?"

She rounded on him in a rage. "No! Not for stealing from my husband, my father, my brother. Not for driving Victor to suicide. Not for any of it! And he wasn't even sorry, not once."

"Hmm," Mr. Jackson murmured. "That's what got her."

His wife, standing beside him, nodded.

Sergeant Nestor said, "So what happened next?"

"I made his acquaintance at the grocery he always went to. Just flirted a little."

Mr. Shapiro's jaw dropped.

Mr. D'Angelo shook his head.

"Then I suggested he bring me to the speakeasy where Ralph worked. Ralph wasn't happy to see me there, but he didn't say anything, just pretended he didn't know me. Then the guy brings out the lighter my brother gave him, cool as a cucumber."

"But you didn't kill him then," said the sergeant.

"No, but that very next day I got a gun. It was so loud in there already you could hardly talk, and I figured on New Year's it'd be even worse."

Sergeant Nestor said, "Is that why you picked that night? The noise?"

She laughed, but it was bitter. "I thought it justice. That was the night my brother shot himself. Now I was gonna shoot him back." She shook her head. "What a night **that** was! Between some old hag trying to get his attention —"

Mrs. Jackson flinched, and he recalled that she and Mabel Franklin were about the same age.

"— and my first husband glaring at me the whole night," she scoffed, "it was a wonder I could get my sleeping powder into his drink without anyone seeing."

Mr. Jackson nodded.

"I suppose you know the rest. He went nighty-night. I shot him and took back my brother's lighter."

"So why didn't you leave?" Sergeant Nestor seemed genuinely curious. "Why'd you stick around?"

"I don't know, to be honest," Pauline said. "I think I wanted to see if he really was dead. So I went to the side there by the curtains and watched. But then he fell on the floor, and everyone started screaming and running! Men were pushing, acting crazy to get out. The whole thing scared me. So I hid behind the curtains and there was a door. But I couldn't make any of the elevators work without a key."

Sergeant Nestor smiled, turning to Mr. D'Angelo. "And you had a key."

The bartender hung his head.

Pauline scowled. "The idiot gave me the wrong one."

"A man was dead!" Mr. D'Angelo held his hand up. "I know, I wasn't to say nothing. But I never seen a man dead before. I dropped the key, my hands shook so. And ... I couldn't think straight. I just wanted her out of there before anyone saw her! I just gave her what I had. Then the police showed up, and that waiter, and —"

"You had to deal with what was happening in front of you." Sergeant Nestor sounded sympathetic. "My forensics man found a key under the bench by the wall the night of the shooting. We were wondering what lock it went to. And I recall you saying the man shouldn't have died there."

Mr. D'Angelo shook his head. "If I'd have known she was going to do that, I'd have called for the bouncers."

Sergeant Nestor turned to Pauline. "So how'd you manage to escape?"

"I found the main laundry. There was a name-tag on the floor beside one of the hampers. I put a fresh uniform on. The elevator guy let me out, and I went home."

"We got a warrant and searched your home when you left for the Auditorium," Sergeant Nestor said, "where we found a black sequined dress with powder burns on it and what I assume is Mr. Boyle's blood."

Mr. Shapiro put his face in his hands. "She didn't come home 'til almost dawn, then rushed to the bathroom and wouldn't tell me where she'd been." He turned to her. "Why wouldn't you tell me?"

"You didn't need to get mixed up in this," she said. "Why'd you have to go all noble and tell them I was at home with you? My friends were ready to say I was with them." She sighed. "I could've handled it."

Mr. Shapiro sat stunned. "Why would I protect you? Because I love you!" He sounded torn, desperate. "I wanted to make them leave us alone!"

The lawyer put his hand on his forehead. "Didn't I tell you not to say anything, sir?"

"I know," Mr. Shapiro said glumly. "But I'm not very good at it."

Epilogue

Mrs. Pauline Shapiro was convicted of the premeditated murder of Mr. Mark Boyle and sentenced to twenty years in prison.

Mr. Ralph D'Angelo visited her every week.

Mr. Milton Shapiro was charged with obstructing a murder investigation. Due to his lack of criminal record (and fine standing in the community), Mr. Shapiro was given probation. Eventually, he divorced Pauline and married a sensible woman closer to his age.

Mr. Montgomery Carlo was charged with violating fire marshal's rulings on safe occupancy, then fined. True to his word, Sergeant Nestor failed to mention the use the room had been put to.

Agents Chapman, Scott, and Haley found the bad liquor. Mr. Russell was sent to Federal prison, which was in an entirely different city. Getting Mr. Russell out of Chicago made several mobsters that were in Chicago breathe a definite sigh of relief.

Mr. Carlo wasn't happy that Sergeant Nestor got to Pauline Shapiro first. Mabel Franklin, on the other hand, visited Pauline Shapiro in prison, and after a bit of sparring, the two became fast friends.

Both KWY Radio and the Chicago Civic Auditorium received generous donations from a Mr. Hector Jackson. It's unclear which of the three was more pleased.

Mr. Jackson began the search for places out West that met everyone's specifications — just in case.

After a few months, Bessie's puppies were old enough to venture out on their own.

The Myriad's Head Clerk Mr. Lee Francis and his wife took home the gold and black spotted puppy for their little son.

Sergeant Nestor's oldest son chose the dark brown puppy for his children.

Duchess Cordelia brought the golden-haired puppy to her suite as her new companion. She purchased specially-made dog boots so that little Bertie might venture out with the dowager on her morning constitutionals, no matter what the weather.

Mrs. Maisy Carlo chose the light brown puppy, who followed her around the Carlo's spacious home and played happily in their equally spacious backyard all the day long.

Miss Trixie Quinlan and her mother decided to stay in Cicero with Trixie's aunt. She and her young cousins were delighted to receive the black female puppy.

When she saw the little dog, Trixie beamed. "I'm going to name her Bessie!"

The next book in the Myriad Mysteries is coming soon!
To learn more about the Myriad Mysteries,
visit Claire Logan's Facebook page,
or follow Claire Logan on Twitter.

Vote on where the next murder will occur at
vote.authorclairelogan.com

Acknowledgements

Thanks so much to Patricia Loofbourrow for the cover design. Also, to my newsletter readers for their help with names for this series.

About the Author

I've loved reading since I can remember! I love puzzles and mysteries and intrigue, and of all the cities I've been to, Chicago is my favorite. My four years living in Chicago during grad school were wonderful. Plus I love history. And wasn't the 1920's wild? I've always wanted to write a fun mystery series set in Chicago and now here's my chance.

Claire Logan is a pen name.

www.ingramcontent.com/pod-product-compliance
Lightning Source LLC
Chambersburg PA
CBHW020820190726
48285CB00006B/2345